PRAISE FOR
THE TEMPTATION SAGA

"Is it hot in here? Congratulations, Ms. Hardt. You dropped me into the middle of a scorching hot story and let me burn."
~ Seriously Reviewed

"I took this book to bed with me and I didn't sleep until 4 a.m. Yes, it's that damn engrossing, so grab your copy now!"
~Whirlwind Books

"Temptation never tasted so sweet... Both tempting, and a treasure... this book held many of the seductive vices I've come to expect from Ms. Hardt's work."
~Bare Naked Words

Tantalizing
MARIA

THE TEMPTATION SAGA
BOOK SEVEN

WATERHOUSE PRESS

Tantalizing

MARIA

THE TEMPTATION SAGA
BOOK SEVEN

For everyone at Waterhouse Press
for believing in this series!

PROLOGUE

The kiss was deep and passionate.

Maria Gomez hadn't known kissing could be so succulent and full of longing, yet so true at the same time. For truth existed in this kiss—a truth she had never felt before.

Never had the juiciest Colorado beef or the richest chocolate tasted as divine as Jeff's mouth on hers.

Truth. Pure truth laced up in craving and wonder.

Maria wasn't all that experienced. She was still a virgin at eighteen, but she'd done her share of kissing. From a shy peck from Leo Martinez when she was fourteen to making out with Greg Black in his car and at myriad parties senior year of high school—yeah, she'd been around the block as far as kissing went.

All of those kisses seemed like the cover band to sit through before Styx finally took the stage.

Jeff Bay? He was definitely Styx.

Jeff was a rebel—a cowboy who wore black leather and rode a Harley Davidson Fat Boy. Tall and built, he could easily model for *GQ*. His walnut hair hung below his ears in lazy waves, and his brown eyes were smoky and smoldering. His full pink lips curved up in a slightly lopsided smile that melted Maria's heart. His skin was the color of peach cream. Maria loved the contrast with her own olive complexion. And when he took off his shirt? *Oh my.* Those broad shoulders and sculpted arms pointed the way to a gorgeous chest and abs.

His nipples were two brown coins nestled in just the right amount of dark hair sprinkled over his chest.

And his butt—covered in jeans that hugged those hips and glutes just right and then snugged around his muscular legs all the way down to his black cowboy boots.

Jeff's full lips slid over hers with the perfect combination of caring softness and reckless abandon. When he probed his tongue between them and entered her mouth, she nearly swooned. He tasted of cinnamon and strawberries, with an accent of wild and savage. His groan vibrated, more than sounded, against her cheeks.

She kissed him back. Not like she'd kissed any other man...no, boy. For in this moment, she knew she'd never kissed a man before. The others had all been boys. And she kissed him back for the first time as a woman, not a girl.

Passion. Eagerness. And agony. Yes, the pure agony of knowing she would never experience another kiss like this.

So this one would have to last. She twirled her tongue with his, lapped up all she could of Jefferson Bay, because he'd never kiss her again. Not silly Maria Gomez. Jeff was twenty-one, a rebel and free spirit. Why he was bothering with her, she had no idea. But she'd question it later.

Right now, she'd enjoy it.

Every single second of it.

He kissed her harder, with raw animal power. She returned his kiss eagerly. Too eager maybe? She didn't care. This might be the only time she'd ever be kissed like this.

When he ripped his lips from hers, her heart sank...but then soared when he smiled down at her with those sparkling brown eyes.

"Damn, Mia."

No one had ever called her Mia before. She'd always been Maria to her mama or sweet pea to her daddy, when he was alive. The endearment from Jeff's lips rang in her ears like joyful bells. She curled her lips upward in a shy smile.

"Nothing to say?"

"What do you want me to say?" she asked coyly.

"Tell me you enjoyed that as much as I did. That you want to kiss me forever. Because damn, honey, I could sure kiss those beautiful lips of yours for even longer than that."

Her lips parted of their own accord.

"God, what a sexy little pout." Jeff shook his head, biting his lower lip. "God damn it all to hell."

And he crushed his mouth to hers again.

CHAPTER ONE

Thirty-Two Years Later

"Mia, and the lovely Angelina." Jefferson Bay's deep voice was laced with sarcasm as he opened the door to his hotel room.

"We need to talk," Maria said.

"Perhaps you and I had best talk in private."

Maria shook her head. "This is Angie's business. After all, she's the one who's about to lose her inheritance."

"So you didn't find a suitable suitor after all?" He clicked his tongue. "How very sad. But how very lucky for me. I now own half a ranch." Grandpa Norman had done one thing right, anyway. He might have disinherited Jeff in favor of his older brother, Wayne, the golden boy, but he left a loophole. Any unmarried daughters couldn't inherit from Wayne, and their portion would revert to any of Norman's living issue.

In other words—Jeff.

His grandfather had been one big male chauvinist pig. And that sad fact was going to work in Jeff's favor.

"You don't own anything yet, Jeff," Maria said, her voice shaking. "Angie still has over a month to get married."

Yes, of course. The codicil. Seemed Grandpa'd had a change of heart, and an unmarried daughter could marry within two months of the golden boy's death and still inherit. "Let me guess. She's holding out for love, right? Love is overrated."

"Is it?" Maria inched closer to him. "Is it really? Don't you remember?"

Jeff stilled his hammering heart. This woman still affected him, but he had to keep his head. "I remember only that you betrayed me by sleeping with my sainted brother. I may have loved you, but you didn't return my love."

Maria's eyes misted. "That's not true, Jeff. You know it's not."

Jeff inhaled, his heart betraying him once again. God, he had loved this woman. More than his own life, he'd loved her. And part of him still did. Beside her stood the daughter who had come between them, the daughter she'd conceived with his brother, the daughter she'd named after his long-dead mother. Angelina was a beautiful girl. Her creamy skin was much like her father's, and her dark hair as lustrous as her mother's. Green eyes, like sparkling emeralds, pierced into him. A twinge of regret niggled at him. She was innocent in all this, after all.

Still, Jeff was entitled to her share of Bay Crossing, and he meant to have it.

"I know only your betrayal, Mia. You slept with my brother and had his child—this beautiful girl in front of us. It's only fitting that I be the means to the end of your and Wayne's love child."

"Damn it, Jeff, you know I was never in love with Wayne."

"Really?" As much as he wanted to believe what she said, he couldn't. "A marriage that lasted this long and produced three children? You're lying."

"You were going to prison."

God, to think of the stupid mistakes he'd made when he was young. But he hadn't killed anyone. "I was innocent! I would have fought, Mia, if I'd thought there was even a ghost of a chance that you and I could be together."

"Why didn't you?"

He raked his fingers through his salt-and-pepper hair. *Because I'd lost everything. I'd lost you.*

"Because you made it clear you thought I was guilty. Dear Granddad had all but hanged me already."

"Why didn't you tell me you were innocent? I would have believed you. I would have stood by you."

"No, you wouldn't have. You had already run to Wayne by then."

"I ran to Wayne because—" She choked into sobs. "My God, I can't do this."

Angie embraced her mother. "She just lost her husband, for God's sake. Can't you take it easy on her? I'm the one you're trying to ruin. Your argument is with me, not her."

Jeff shook his head. "How little you know. You've told your children nothing of me, have you, Mia? Yet you stand there and tell me you had feelings for me all that time ago." He stifled the emotional turmoil of watching the traitorous woman cradle his niece, and then he glared at Angie. "I can hurt your lovely mother by hurting you. Icing on the cake."

"No, Jeff," Maria gasped out. "I won't let you do this to her."

He smiled. Not a nice smile. He knew it. He wasn't feeling overly nice right now. "I don't see that you have much of a choice."

Angie spoke then. "I'm sorry, Mama. I've already told you I'm not marrying Frank. And there isn't time for me to fall in love."

Good. Don't marry Frank. Don't marry anyone. I deserve

a piece of Grandpa's pie.

"You're right, Angie." Maria steadied herself, taking some of her weight off Angie. "You're not going to marry Frank. You're not going to marry anyone you don't love just to get a piece of land."

Works for me. "Then I think we're done here," Jeff said, moving toward the door. "Nice to see you, ladies."

Maria rushed forward and pounded her fists onto Jeff's chest. Jeff startled when his skin tightened. Even in anger, her touch still moved him. How he longed to grab Maria and drag her into his arms.

"Damn it, Jeff, we are not done here!"

"Mama?" Angie said, inching toward them.

"You won't do this to her. I swear you won't!"

Jeff steadied himself and gripped Maria's shoulders, forcing himself not to cave into the desire touching her evoked in him. "I stand to gain everything by doing this."

"But you can't."

"You keep saying that, Mia." He shook her and immediately regretted it. He'd never gotten rough with any woman, and he didn't plan to start now. "Why? Why can't I? Why shouldn't I take what should have been rightfully mine in the first place?"

Maria whipped her hands upward and grabbed both sides of Jeff's face. So warm, so sweet. And she smelled the same, like wild berries and sweet vanilla. He forced himself not to inhale.

Then she plowed into him with her chocolate gaze. "Because she's *your* daughter, God damn it!"

Angie went pale. "Mama?" Her voice squeaked.

"I'm sorry, Angelina. I shouldn't have blurted it out like

that, but it's true. Wayne Bay is not your biological father. Jefferson Bay is."

Jeff's knees weakened and threatened to collapse under him. "You're lying, Mia, and it won't work."

"It's not a lie, you fool. To be honest, I'm surprised none of you suspected it at the time. If it's proof you want, you and Angie go for a DNA test. I guarantee the results will show she's yours."

His muscles tensed, and bile rose in his throat. This could not be happening. This child? His? This woman? His daughter? This beautiful girl... She was...what? Thirty-two then? "How? Why?"

"Didn't you wonder why I suddenly had an interest in your brother when I'd had none previously? Didn't you wonder when my baby girl was born a month early? No, none of you gave it a second thought. It seemed so obvious to me, but neither you, Wayne, nor your grandfather batted an eye over it."

The words rang in Jeff's ears. First they made sense, and then they didn't, and then he was sure this had to be a dream... and then he knew it wasn't. This was real.

"I think I might be sick," Angie said.

Maria rushed to her and helped her to one of the queen beds in the hotel room. "I'm so sorry, Angie. I never meant for you to find out like this. I never meant for you to find out at all."

"At all?" Angie blinked her eyes. "How could you? How could you lie to me all these years?"

"I'm sorry."

"Daddy never knew? Never suspected?"

"If he did I didn't know it."

Jeff cleared his throat. *Get a grip.* "Mia, I demand an explanation right now."

"Yes, I owe you both that much." Maria sat down on the bed and took Angie's hand in her own. She rubbed it lightly. "I found out I was pregnant after you were arrested. With all your trouble with the law, I assumed you were guilty."

Jeff's heart began the stampede again. Ire flamed within him. "After everything we shared, how could you know me so little? Do you really think I could kill someone?"

"No." Maria shook her head. "But I knew you'd go to prison for a long time anyway. I figured you'd had a hand in it. After all, it wasn't the first time you'd been at the scene of a crime. There was no way around it. You had a record. I needed to make sure my baby—*our* baby—had a chance at the life and the name she deserved. So I seduced Wayne and, a month later, told him the child was his."

Jefferson plunked down onto the other bed. "Oh, Mia."

"I'm not proud of it. But he adored your daughter, Jeff. She was his favorite. She wanted for nothing while he was alive."

"Oh, Mia, you don't understand." He lowered his heavy head into his hands. All these years. He'd gone to prison, for God's sake. To prison, because he thought he'd lost everything.

Maria gripped Angie's hand tighter. "What? What are you not telling me?"

"I only pleaded guilty because I thought you'd betrayed me. I'd been ready to fight. To fight for us. To do anything to get out of the mess I'd gotten myself into and go straight for you. I was going to get a job, make my own way, prove to my grandfather that I wasn't the fuck up he thought I was. I was ready to prove it to you. For us. Mia...why? You were the love of my life," Jeff said, his voice wavering. "All this time, I had a child. A child I never knew."

"Mama?"

"Yes, Angie?"

"Harper and Catie?"

"They're your father's. Er...Wayne's. I never strayed during our marriage. Not once."

"And I—"

"Jeff is your biological father. I'm so sorry. I didn't mean for you to find out this way. Or to find out at all—"

"You planned to keep this child from me forever?" Jeff's voice had deepened, tinted with more anger, almost rage. Yes, he was angry. This woman had stolen his life. "Didn't you think I had the right to know I had a daughter?"

"And didn't you think I had the right to know who my real father was?" Angie demanded.

Maria's weight sank down farther into the bed, as though she wanted to melt into it, to melt away and never return.

"Angie, you *had* a real father. A real father who adored you."

"Would he have adored me so much if he'd known the truth?"

"I don't know. But what does it matter?"

"What does it matter? Are you serious?"

For Christ's sake. The two of them were going on and on as if he weren't in the room. "And what about me, Mia?" Jeff interjected. "What about me?"

"You were serving a life sentence. What would you have done with a child? What would I have done as a single mother?"

"You never loved Daddy," Angie choked out.

"He never loved me either."

Angie shook her head, rubbing her cheeks against the hotel pillow. "You shouldn't have married him. He deserved to be loved."

Marie held her—*their*—daughter's hand. "I did it for you, Angie. For *you*. Can't anyone see that?"

"Bullshit." Angie sat up. "You did it for yourself. Your boyfriend was going to prison and you were stuck pregnant. You trapped an innocent man into a marriage neither of you wanted. I'll never forgive you for this. Never!"

"Angie, please."

"The girl's right, Mia." Jeff tried to defuse his rage. "What you did was wrong on so many levels."

Maria sighed. "I'm not arguing that point."

"Christ, Mia. I loved you. I would have done anything for you. For our child."

"You couldn't escape a prison sentence."

"But I would have fought. I could have turned state's evidence. I could have gotten a better lawyer. I could have..." *Could have done so many things...*

"I had to make a decision quickly. A decision that I thought was best for my child. You'll be happy to know, Jeff, that Angie never wanted for anything. She had everything a little girl could want."

"Except her real father," Jeff said.

"You can't take her inheritance. You can't do this to your own daughter."

"She's not my daughter." Jeff stalked forward. "You took her from me and gave her to my brother. My sainted brother. He had everything. He was the older. He had Grandpa's love and devotion. He had everything I could never have, except you. I had you. But you took that away and gave yourself to him. You gave my child to him!"

"He wasn't the one I loved, Jeff. You were."

No, her words would not sway him. They were nothing but lies. "You think that matters now?"

"Yes, it should matter. The fact that she's yours should matter. Please don't take her ranch away from her."

"The ranch is mine. She can have it when I'm dead. Now the two of you get the hell out of my hotel room." He stormed across the carpet and opened the door.

CHAPTER TWO

A Year and a Half Later

"How many more times"—Maria Bay shook her head—"are we going to have this same damned argument, Jeff? I don't know what you want me to say anymore. I've apologized. I've explained. I've done the best I can for the last year to make this up to you. Yet you still stay in that tiny house. You won't even let me cook you dinner."

Jefferson Bay regarded the beautiful woman who was his sister-in-law and the mother of his only child. Her onyx hair still fell past her shoulders in bouncing waves—just like it always had. Her warm brown eyes gazed up at him with searching innocence—just as they had thirty-three years ago.

He inhaled to clear his mind. Maria was no innocent.

Still, his heart roared at him to grab her and kiss her the way he used to—the way he had when he was a young man in love for the first time.

The only time.

He'd made a sort of nervous peace with his daughter, Angelina. She hadn't even known he'd existed until a year ago when her father—Jeff's brother—had passed on. Wayne Bay had died never knowing that his younger brother had fathered his oldest child. Now, Jeff and Angie were building a relationship as father-uncle and daughter. It wasn't strong yet, by any means. Angie called him Jeff. She said Dad or Uncle Jeff didn't feel right to her. Understandable. Wayne and Maria hadn't ever told the kids they had an uncle, let alone that he was Angie's real father. Nope, Jeff had been a convicted felon serving time. A true skeleton in the closet.

With Angie, Jeff had patience. She and her husband were expecting their first child. Jeff was going to be a grandfather—a pretty daunting concept to a man who'd only been a father for the past year. He was treading carefully with Angie. He was lucky she spoke to him at all after he'd threatened to take her inheritance when Wayne had died. Not one of his finer moments. She was innocent in all this, after all. She wasn't the one who'd betrayed him and lied to him for three decades.

Nope. That honor went to her mother.

Maria. Not so innocent.

His first and only love still captivated him, though. He couldn't take his eyes from her when she was near. Even as he worked on the ranch, when she came near he found his gaze drawn to her flowing hair, her curvy body that looked sumptuous in simple jeans and a western shirt. All those years in prison he'd never forgotten her, no matter how hard he tried. He'd taught himself not to think of her during the daylight hours. And even at night, as he fell into slumber on his cot, listening to the muffled sounds of inmates snoring and crying, he'd forced his mind to other things. Much better than imagining what they'd had, or rather, what he'd *thought* they had.

Or worse yet, imagining her in his brother's bed.

But sleep... That was a different story. She'd haunted him in his dreams. She stormed in and took possession of him, as if to say, "You can't shut me out, no matter how hard you try, Jeff. I'm here in your head and your heart. I'm part of your very soul, and I'll never leave. Never."

He feared he'd never be free of her. Much as he tried, he couldn't harden his heart.

And now here she stood, hands on her hips, fire darting from her dark brown eyes.

"I guess you'll have to tell *me* how long this will go on, Mia. How long does it take to get over thirty years of lies?"

Her eyes softened back to their warm chocolate. "I don't understand you, Jeff. Sometimes you're caring and warm, and I think you're coming around, and then you go cold again."

He couldn't deny her words. The truth was he wanted her back in his life. Back in his bed. But prison had hardened him. He didn't want to live a life of resentment. He'd been there, done that. The result wasn't pretty. Yet whenever he moved forward to smile, to take Mia into his arms, to *forgive*, unwanted images popped into his mind.

Perfect Wayne. Five years Jeff's senior, Wayne had been the golden boy. The apple of Grandpa Norman's eye. Jeff had never been able to compare, so he'd gone his own way and taken a path of self-destruction.

Until he'd met his Mia.

God, no. Not my Mia. She hasn't been my Mia for a very long time.

He'd been ready to change, to have a life with her, until she betrayed him with his own brother.

That he couldn't get past.

"Are you going to answer me or just stand there?" Mia's voice rose. "I invited you to dinner, damn it. You've been here a year and eaten with me only a handful of times."

Still he didn't speak. Didn't even nod.

"We agreed when I invited you to live here on the ranch that we'd try to rebuild our friendship. I haven't asked for anything more. But you refuse even that."

Jeff cleared his throat. "I'm trying, Mia."

"Really? Could've fooled me." She turned and then glanced back at him over her shoulder. "Dinner will be on the table at seven p.m. Angie and Rafe are in town and would like to see you. I've invited Harper and Amber too."

Angie was coming? He'd known she was coming to town but didn't realize she was here yet. That was a horse of a different color. He nodded. "I'll be there. Thank you for the invite."

He inhaled and willed his body to stop the inner quivering that jumbled his insides whenever Maria was near. And he went back to work.

★ ★ ★

"You have to give him time, Mama," Harper Bay said. "Think of what he's lost."

"I know very well what he's lost." Maria filled the coffeepot with water and poured it into the machine. "Do you think I haven't lived with that myself for the last thirty years? Not a day went by that the guilt didn't eat me alive."

"You never showed it. We never knew."

"Of course I never showed it. I had a husband, children, a family to take care of. You all deserved my best."

"We got that."

Harper warmed Maria's heart. God bless her wonderful son. She *had* been a good mother, and Wayne had been an incredible father, even though he'd spoiled Angelina rotten. But she was fine now, happily married and expecting. "Thank you, hon."

"But you had us all those years. You had Angie. All that time, he was rotting in prison. You can't compare your two lives. It's apples and oranges. Really, it's apples and crap, to tell the truth."

Maria nodded. Her son was right, of course. Even though she and Wayne hadn't been in love, they'd had a good life. Their children had grown up happy and secure. Jeff, on the other hand, had lived a nightmare in prison.

"I know, Harp. I know." What more could she say? She was lucky Harper had taken the news—that his sister was his half-sister/half-cousin and that his mother had lied to his father all those years—so well.

If she could erase the pain of Jeff's past she would, but she couldn't. They had to move forward. Besides, things couldn't have worked out any differently. If they had, she wouldn't have the amazing son standing before her now, or her youngest child, Catie.

"He's still here," Harper said. "He could have left, but he hasn't. And he's earning his own way. We've told him we'd take care of him, give him what should rightfully be his."

"He's too proud. He needs to work for his supper." And work he did. Harper told her daily what a great job he was doing, how he worked harder than any of the other hands. And Lord God, it showed. In the year since he'd been at Cha Cha Ranch, he'd tightened up those muscles and had the body he'd had at twenty-one. He was just as handsome, if not more so, with his wavy dark hair now sprinkled with a little salt.

"That's a good thing, Mama. There's a good man inside him. He just needs to get through this. And he will. Look how well he and Angie are doing."

Maria nodded, thankful. In some small way, Jeff's

presence was easing the pain of Wayne's passing on Angie. Ironically, Angie had been the closest to Wayne, closer than either of his biological children.

"He'll be here in an hour for supper. I guess I'd best get busy."

"What are you making?"

"Beef empanadas."

Harper laughed. "Any man who can resist your beef empanadas isn't worth having around."

★ ★ ★

Thirty-Three Years Earlier

"See something you like?"

Jeff broke his gaze on the hot little Latina number and turned to Max, who'd just finished gassing up his bike. The hottie and her friend were across the street in the high school parking lot. "Nope. Just admiring the view. I don't do high school girls. Jailbait and all."

"The one with the long hair? I can't remember her name, but I know she's eighteen."

Jeff's heart lurched. "Yeah? How do you know?"

"That's my cousin Shelley she's talking to."

"Really? So you know her?"

"Nope. Shelley's mom and my mom don't talk. Some stupid-ass sisters' feud. But I met that friend of hers a while back, before the big falling out, and Shelley mentioned that she was exactly a month older than her friend. Shelley turned eighteen almost two months ago, so do the math. She's grown up damned nice, I'll say."

★ ★ ★

"He's bad news, Maria," Rochelle Harte said. "He's always in trouble. I heard he held up Moon Liquors last weekend."

"Heard from whom?" Maria had locked her gaze on the tall biker with dark hair and eyes. His face was beautiful—angelic almost—but in a completely masculine way. God, he screamed man with a capital M.

"Just heard. He's part of that Rebel Riders gang."

"Do you know his name?"

"Bay. Jeff Bay."

"Not the Bays of Bay Crossing Ranch?" Maria's heart nearly skipped a beat.

"Yup. The one and only. Though from what I hear he's been disinherited and darn near disowned. Plus he's too old for you. In his twenties."

"That's not too old. I'm legal."

"Right. What's he going to want with a high school student?"

"We graduate in two weeks, Shelley. Sheesh."

"What are you looking around for, anyway? You and Greg are practically engaged."

"That may be what he thinks, but no, we're not." She held up her hand. "Do you see a ring on this finger? I'm not ready to settle down, anyway. College is going to be a blast."

"Yeah, it is. So what are you making moon eyes over Jeff Bay for? He's no college man. We're all going to CU together, including Greg."

"Yeah." Try as she might, Maria couldn't get excited over another four years with Greg Black. He was handsome, and he was smart, and he was captain of the football team...yada yada yada. He was also boring. All they did was make out. He'd tried many times to go further, but she wouldn't. "I'm holding off until I'm eighteen," she'd say.

That excuse no longer held water. She'd been eighteen for nearly a month now. Luckily, they were all busy with finals and the impending graduation, and Greg hadn't been pestering her. But it would happen, and soon.

Truth be told, she didn't want to lose her virginity to Greg Black. He wasn't the one. She knew that. She didn't know how she knew, but she knew.

She was still staring at the gorgeous cowboy on a motorcycle when his dark gaze suddenly met hers. His eyes were laced with hunger. Was he actually melting her clothes off her body?

She gulped. "Oh, God."

"What?" Shelley said.

Maria didn't answer. Jeff Bay's full lips curved into a lazy grin, his gaze never leaving her. Damn, why hadn't she worn a nicer blouse today? Suddenly her Styx T-shirt felt infantile.

"Earth to Maria."

Maria shook her head quickly and turned back to Shelley. "Sorry. What did you say?"

"Nothing that matters. Get your head out of the clouds. We're going to be late for class."

Class? Heck, they were graduating in two weeks. She had a three point nine grade point average. She'd already been accepted to college. Who needed to go to class?

"Go ahead. I need to run back to the car. Forgot one of my notebooks."

"Okay." Shelley shrugged and walked toward the school

building.

Slowly, Maria ambled toward her car. All her notebooks were in the backpack around her shoulders, of course, but she'd had to stall. Couldn't bear to leave just yet.

Shelley was right. Jeff Bay wouldn't give her the time of day. Sure, he'd look to his heart's content. Most guys did. She was used to that—the power of long dark hair and large breasts. It had been going on since she was fourteen. But for one more minute—sixty more seconds—she wanted to dream that the gorgeous bad boy on the bike might be hers someday.

Maria fumbled in her car for a few minutes and then walked toward the school, turning her back to the gorgeous biker.

God, what an idiot I am. He is so not my type.

The slow thundering of a motorcycle engine revved up behind her, and she gulped and turned her head. Next to her, mounted on his bike, was her dream man.

He turned to her, his eyes blazing.

"Hop on."

Maria didn't think. She just hopped on, happy to obey his command. No helmet, no leather jacket—she had no protective gear at all except the pack full of books on her back.

And she didn't care one bit.

Jeff rode slowly through the high school parking lot and out onto the street, and then he gunned it onto the highway.

Freedom. Exhilaration. Maria had never felt anything like it. The wind tossed her hair about, sure to make it a rat's nest to comb out later, but she didn't care. Her eyelashes blew against her eyelids. If only she could reach into her backpack for her sunglasses.

Oh, well, next time.

Would there be a next time?

Yes. She'd make sure of it. She hadn't had her last taste of a Harley.

Or of Jeff Bay, she hoped.

They screamed down the highway toward the countryside. She had no idea where they were going, and while that fact normally would have bothered her, it didn't at this moment. All that mattered was the vibrating seat between her thighs and the strong, hard back of the man in front of her. She wanted to ride like the wind.

For a half hour they rode, until he finally got off the highway, trekked down a county road, and stopped at a little mom-and-pop shop on the corner.

He helped her off the bike and met her gaze. "Hey," he said.

"Hey."

"You want something to drink?"

She swallowed. Yeah, she was parched. Plus this gave her a chance to dig for her sunglasses so her eyelids wouldn't turn inside out again. She nodded.

"Coke?" He grinned. "Diet coke?"

"Just water, actually. I can give you some money."

"Nah, it's on me. No worries." He ambled into the shop.

Maria followed him and headed toward the ladies' room. When she looked in the mirror, she nearly had a coronary. Her hair was a mass of tangles and waves. She dug into her backpack for her brush and tugged it through her hair until the last snarl was gone. Then she laughed out loud. It would just happen again when she went back on the bike.

And she had every intention of getting back on that bike.

She took a moment to look at her reflection. Her cheeks

were pink. Damn, they were glowing. And her lips were ruby red. Riding a motorcycle agreed with her.

Or Jeff Bay agreed with her.

She walked back out to find Jeff waiting with her drink by the bike. He had removed his T-shirt, and his tanned, broad chest glistened with perspiration. *Oh, God.*

"So what's your name, beautiful?" he asked.

Her cheeks heated. Damn, they were already ruddy from the ride. "Maria," she said quickly.

He smiled. "Mia?"

"No, Maria."

"Oh, okay." He reached toward her and trailed one finger down the curve of her cheek. "I like Mia better. It fits you."

Had his finger been a lighted match? He'd left a trail of sparks in his wake. She hadn't thought her cheeks could burn any hotter, but they did.

"I'm Jeff. Jeff Bay."

She gulped. "Yeah, I know."

"So you've heard of me?"

"No, not really. My friend knew who you were."

"Well, that's good enough for me." He smiled again. "How old are you, Mia?"

She swallowed. "Eighteen."

His grin was wide and showed perfect white teeth. "Good. That's real good." He leaned down and touched his lips to hers.

The kiss was deep and passionate...

CHAPTER THREE

Jeff finished currying the last mare and stretched. Amazing how much he enjoyed ranch work after all these years. He'd rebelled against it with a vengeance on Grandpa's ranch all those years ago, preferring instead to hang out with those criminal "friends" of his. He'd found out the hard way that they weren't his friends.

He'd found out the hard way about Maria, too.

She was trying. He'd give her credit for that. She certainly didn't owe him anything after what he'd threatened to do to Angie. *Hell, I guess we're even now. She betrayed me with my own brother and kept a child from me for thirty-two years.* Course he'd been a loser back then and had done time to prove it. Maybe he'd gotten what he deserved.

He had an income now. Harper, his nephew, who legally owned Cha Cha Ranch now that Wayne had passed, paid him a good salary. Plus, Harper let him use the small house Angie had lived in before she married Rafe and moved to the western slope to manage Bay Crossing. He was lucky his nephew hadn't booted him out after he'd tried to take Angie's inheritance.

But Jeff hadn't been able to go through with it, especially after Maria had told him Angie was his daughter and not Wayne's. He'd never imagined they'd created a child during those few nights of nirvana. He hadn't lived as a monk, but damn if those times with Mia hadn't been heavenly. He hadn't had anything comparable since then.

He feared he never would.

It was a loner's life for him from now on. Well, not exactly a loner. Angie had let him into her life and had promised to let him be a grandpa to her baby when it came. He counted his lucky stars for that. Harper and Catie had accepted him as well. Harp said he had a job and a place to live as long as he wanted, and it wasn't just nepotism. Harper made no bones about the fact that Jeff worked harder than any other hand on the ranch.

"Aw, hell," he said out loud, looking at his watch. Time to go to dinner at Maria's house. He didn't have a lot of time to clean up, but he'd go home and shower anyway. His daughter was visiting.

★ ★ ★

"For goodness' sake, Mama, he'll be here." Angie breathed out loudly. "This baby has determined that my bladder is a punching bag. Excuse me." She left the table.

"The man can't be on time to save his own soul," Maria said to Harper, his wife, Amber, and Angie's husband, Rafe. They sat around Maria's round table in the kitchen. No sense using the formal dining room for family. They were all more comfortable here in her big country kitchen.

Jeff stumbled in a few minutes later, his hair damp, looking luscious in jeans and a clean white shirt. "Hey," he said, "sorry I'm late."

Maria pursed her lips, but the young people all smiled.

"Not a problem, Uncle Jeff," Harper said.

Jeff nodded. "I'm going to call the vet in the morning.

The gray gelding's frog is looking a little inflamed."

Harper nodded. "Silverstreak? Yeah, he's had a chronic problem for a while now. Give Annie a call."

"I will." He looked around the room. "Where's Angie?"

Rafe laughed. "One guess."

Jeff smiled. "Bathroom?"

"Yup."

So he's really just going to stand there and not speak to me? Maria tapped her foot. *Well, fine then. Two can play this game.*

Angie returned to the table and Maria sat down without nodding to Jeff. He sat down, once everyone else was seated, next to Angie.

Harper and Rafe began a conversation about the steers at Bay Crossing, and Jeff joined in. Maria had been a rancher's wife for over thirty years, so she knew a thing or two about the business. But she kept to herself, moving her food around her plate like a little kid who was trying to make it look like he was eating something he didn't want to eat.

She loved beef empanadas, but her stomach felt like lead at the moment. She couldn't force herself to take even one bite.

Jeff smiled at the others, even chuckled a time or two. Why? Why was he able to get close to her children but not to her? How long would he make her pay for her mistake?

Thirty years.

The words popped into her head without so much as a warning.

Thirty years.

The amount of time Jeff had spent in prison for a crime he hadn't committed. He'd paid dearly for his mistake of hanging with criminals when he was young. Thirty damn years. That was a hell of a long time—more than half his life so far.

Would he make her pay for her mistake for thirty years?

Her eyes began to mist, but she inhaled and quickly stopped the tears from forming.

Fine. Thirty years. She could wait.

She had no choice.

★ ★ ★

Thirty-Three Years Earlier
That little Mia is something else.

Jeff had been around the block more than a few times, but never had a kiss affected him like this. Mia was a temptress, a siren, wrapped up in an innocent-looking package of beautiful dark hair, flawless olive skin, and an amazing body. Clearly liked Styx, according to her T-shirt. Only the best band in the universe. And those cherry-red lips. God, had that thought really entered his head? *Cherry-red?* Since when did he notice the color of a woman's lips? When they were full and sexy and begging to be kissed, that's when.

He hadn't meant to kiss her out of the blue, but hell, he hadn't been able to stop. She'd looked at him with that sexy little pout and he had to have those lips on his. Simple as that.

She knew how to kiss too, had sunk into him like the siren she was.

He kissed her like he'd never kissed a woman before. He wanted to mark her as his, claim her.

God damn, he'd just met her.

His cock rose inside his jeans. He loved kissing, but it usually took a little more than a first kiss to get a rise. But this was no normal first kiss.

This was a kiss to cherish, to savor—it was a kiss he'd judge all other kisses against in his lifetime.

And at that moment, he didn't ever want to kiss another woman in his lifetime.

Her sweet little moan sang into his mouth like a bluebird's song. He twirled his tongue around hers, swirled it over her teeth and gums, the insides of her cheeks. He wanted to taste every last millimeter of her sweet mouth.

When his lungs required air, he forced his mouth from hers, took a breath, and then rained tiny kisses over her smooth cheeks and neck. She smelled of wild berries and sweet vanilla. God, he could live on that aroma. He could live on her kisses alone and die a happy man.

Her skin quivered under his lips.

"Oh, God," she said softly.

His heart hammered. Her skin was like velvet beneath his fingers, his lips. Soft, warm, tan velvet. He knew nothing about her, only that she was eighteen and delicious to kiss.

She was young and probably not that experienced. And she was into him, and into this kiss. If he were a different kind of man, he'd go for it—screw her brains out and leave without finding out anything about her. But though he scoffed at authority and rebelled against the law, he respected the fairer sex. His mama had died when he was only five, but he remembered her somewhat—soft and feminine yet protective and fierce when it came to her boys. His daddy had treated his mama like a treasure. And she had been a treasure. Angelina. Her name was Angelina.

Mia.

Just as soft and feminine of a name. He'd take care of his

Mia.

His Mia?

What the hell? Though it pained him, he removed his lips from the creamy skin of her neck.

He regarded her, her eyes closed, her breaths coming in rapid puffs. God, she was the picture of beauty and innocence all rolled up into one.

"What would you like to do, Mia?"

"Kiss some more?" she said shyly.

Damn. I'd like that too. His cock strained against his jeans. "Nothing I'd like better," he said, "but if I keep kissing you like that I might not be able to stop. Where do you live, anyway?"

"In town." She looked down, clearing her throat. "Near the railroad tracks."

Not a great neighborhood. Poor thing was embarrassed.

"Okay. When do you need to be home?"

"Well, Mama thinks I'm at school, so not until around three."

"You graduating?"

"Yeah. Going to CU in the fall with some of my friends."

College. Wayne had gone to college. Jeff's ACT scores had been darn near perfect, but he'd chosen to skip out on further education. That had been the beginning of the end with Grandpa Norm.

Nah, he was kidding himself. The beginning of the end had come senior year of high school when he'd been arrested for drunk driving with his buddies. After the five-day lecture and horse whipping, Jeff had rebelled against everything, including college. And that's when Grandpa disinherited him.

Sure, he could have kissed ass and gotten back in the

will. He could have started college a semester or a year later. Sometimes he played the "what if?" game, but what good did it do? He'd chosen his path. Or his path had chosen him.

Sounded better that way. Then he didn't have to take the blame for his stupid-ass life.

Mia.

Somehow, his stupid-ass life seemed more purposeful when he looked into the warm eyes of this pretty girl he'd just met.

"How'd you like to go for a long ride with me?"

She blinked, and those long onyx lashes lay on her cheeks like fine silk threads. "Um, sure. I'd love to ride. Your bike is amazing."

"Let's go back in the store. We'll get you something for your hair so it doesn't get all out of control again. A rubber band or something. You'll be more comfortable."

"Sure. Okay."

"I wish I had a helmet for you." Why was he feeling so protective? "I'll bring one the next time we go on a ride."

"Why? You don't wear one."

"No, I don't." But he'd start. Suddenly, not having his brains glopped all over concrete appealed to him. "I have a few at home. Next time, we both wear them."

"Okay."

"In fact, we'll stop at my place and get them. How's that sound?"

"Sure. Okay."

He chuckled. "You know any other words, Mia?"

She smiled and her eyes sparkled. "Sure."

He grabbed her hand, and a tingle shot up his arm. "Come on. Let's get something for your hair."

CHAPTER FOUR

"Come on, bitch, open up, or I'll fucking jam this fork into your eye."

"Please. Please. Don't...mmmfff."

"Yeah, bitch. Take it all. You love my big cock shoved in your throat, don't you?"

The boy, who looked no older than nineteen, pleaded with Jeff with his eyes. Help me. Help me.

Three other inmates held the boy down while Big Chuck forced his penis into the boy's mouth.

Jeff lunged forward and grabbed Big Chuck around the neck.

They toppled to the ground. The boy turned and threw up in the gravel.

"You're lookin' for trouble, Bay," Big Chuck said. "You don't want little peewee here to take my cock? You can take it for him."

Jeff punched Big Chuck in the gut. The large man let out an oof.

"You just bought yourself a heap of trouble."

Chuck's minions grabbed Jeff by the collar and forced him to the ground. Gravel sanded his face as one asshole rubbed it into the dirt. Both his arms were pinned, and his pants and boxers were forced from his legs. He lay helpless, spread eagled on the pavement.

The guards circled the grounds, but no help would come.

They turned a blind eye. What the fuck did they care? The prisoners were nothing but animals to them—animals to be hosed down and slopped a couple of times a day.

No help would come from the other inmates either. They all knew better. Look out for number one, or your number'd be up pretty quickly.

"I'm going to fuck you, Bay." Big Chuck's voice slithered around him like a cunning rattlesnake. "And you're gonna love it, you interfering little pussy."

★ ★ ★

Jeff woke with a start and sat straight up in bed. Cold sweat trickled down his forehead, his chest. His heart thundered against his sternum. His sheets were clammy and damp. The nightmare was always the same. Just as Big Chuck was about to rape him, he woke up.

Jeff closed his eyes.

Thank God it was only a nightmare. The scenario had never taken place. He'd learned to avoid the bulls in prison. He was big enough, strong enough, and though his pretty face had made him a target when he first went to Canon City, his strong fists had protected him. That and the few good friends he made early on, thank God.

Though he longed to intervene during one of the many rapes he witnessed, he'd learned not to. He suffered a beating that landed him in the infirmary for two weeks the one and only time he'd tried, with the boy from his nightmare. The poor boy had been gangbanged anyway for Jeff's efforts.

The guilt still ate Jeff alive. All those poor boys, and he hadn't been able to help. Hadn't been able to do anything except close his eyes to the horror around him.

He looked at the clock on his night table. Four a.m. Well, might as well get up. The alarm would go off in an hour anyway. Funny, he hadn't had this particular nightmare in prison. He hadn't had to—the nightmare had been all around him. Each day was a new threat, a new horror.

No, back in prison, his nights had been reserved for Mia. She'd haunted his dreams, no matter how hard he tried to force her from his mind.

Now he'd been on her ranch for nearly a year. He'd healed a lot, pushed a lot of the resentment from his mind. Big brother Wayne had led the life Jeff should have had with Mia and their daughter. But he'd forgiven Wayne. Truly. Best not to resent the dead. What good did it do? He'd decided when he gave Angie back her inheritance that he didn't want to live a life of resentment and become a bitter old man.

He truly didn't want that.

But he couldn't chase the nightmares away.

And then there was Mia.

Every time she came near him he wanted her more, longed for his lips on hers, his body entwined with hers. If possible, she was even more beautiful now than she'd been thirty years ago. She'd aged gracefully. Her hair was still black as night, and her face was still creamy and tan, with only the slightest laugh wrinkles around her eyes. Obviously, she'd laughed a lot over the years. She'd had a happy life. He'd stopped resenting that. He was glad she'd been happy with Wayne. No reason why everyone had to suffer.

And he was extremely grateful that his daughter had been happy, had lived the good life she'd deserved. He owed Wayne for that one. It was a debt he'd never be able to repay.

Yes, Mia. She invaded his thoughts once again. She most likely always would.

Her body was still perfect, just slightly curvier around the belly. She'd had three kids, of course.

God, he still wanted her. Had never stopped wanting her.

And she wanted him. A few months ago, she had finally come to him. She'd appeared one night at the foot of his bed.

She was a vision, her perfect body clothed in only peach-colored satin and lace. "I'm sorry for intruding, Jeff. I still have Angie's old key."

He shielded his eyes against her luminescence. For that's what it was. She lit up the dark bedroom, as if the creamy-orange fabric reflected her light from within.

"It's okay, Mia. What do you want?"

She edged a knee onto the bed. "I think you know, Jeff. I'm dressed this way for a reason."

"Something from your drawers, I gather, that you used to wear for Wayne?"

She closed her eyes for a moment and inhaled. "No. Something I bought today. In town. Just for you. I never wore stuff like this for Wayne. We didn't have that kind of relationship. We weren't...in love."

He nodded. And gulped. "So you've told me."

"How long are you going to make me wait, Jeff? You say you've forgiven me, that you hold no resentment. You're forging a relationship with your daughter and your niece and nephew. They're growing to love you." She came closer, stroked his forearm.

Wild stallions trampled inside him. His cock roared to life.

"Why not me, Jeff? Why can't we have what we once

did?"

So many reasons—reasons he could never divulge to her. Reasons that wouldn't make sense to her. They made sense only to him.

"I know you still love me, Jeff. I can see it in your eyes every time you look at me."

He said nothing. What could he say? Of course he still loved her. He'd never stopped.

"And you know I love you. My whole life, I've loved only one man. You."

Ripples of fire blazed up his arm as she continued to stroke him. His cock hardened to granite inside his boxers. Thank God for the covers.

"We could have that life now. The one we used to talk about. Do you remember?"

Remember? Those memories played like an epic movie in his mind. Over and over again. God, yes, he remembered.

But he didn't nod. He still said nothing.

"You haven't denied that you love me."

Of course he hadn't. He couldn't.

"Could you say it, Jeff? Please? Just say you love me. I need to hear it."

His lips trembled. The words formed on his vocal cords but stayed lodged in his throat. If he said it, if he let those three little words out, he wouldn't be able to stop himself. He'd grab her and kiss her—God, the memory of her kisses still brought him to his knees. Then he'd make love to her. He wouldn't be able to stop himself.

So he had to stop now.

He stayed silent.

One solitary tear dripped down Mia's smooth cheek,

glistening in the moonlight streaming in from the window.

She turned and left.

How he'd wanted to take her in his arms.

But he couldn't. He just couldn't.

He wasn't sure he'd ever be able to.

She'd apologized profusely the next day for her wanton behavior. Yes, she'd actually used the word wanton, his Mia. The few times she'd brought up their relationship since then, he'd lied to her that he still couldn't forgive her betrayal, as he had this morning.

Truth be told, he'd forgiven her as soon as he'd moved onto the ranch. He'd forgiven Wayne too. Problem was, one person still existed whom he couldn't forgive.

Himself.

★ ★ ★

He still loved her. Maria knew it with all her heart. But something was keeping him from her. He'd gotten close to Angie, to Harper and Catie, even to some of the other folks around town.

Yet he still couldn't forgive her.

Well, could she blame him? She hadn't wanted to seduce Wayne and pass off Angie as his child, but she'd been eighteen and penniless, from a modest—okay, crappy—part of town. She'd felt she had no choice. Between a rock and a hard place. What else could she have done? Angie had deserved better. Truly, she had done it for Angie and not herself. That was the God's honest truth, no matter what Jeff insisted on thinking.

She'd done the right thing by inviting him here to live. He had nothing, after all, and what had been Wayne's was rightfully half his. He was doing the job of two men around here, according to Harper, and he was good at it, seemed to enjoy it.

Seeing him with Angie warmed her heart. They were becoming close. Would they ever have a true father and daughter relationship? She didn't know, but she hoped so. They were gaining ground every day. Angie had forgiven Maria, and she'd forgiven Jeff as well.

Why wouldn't *he* forgive her?

She cringed as that fateful night surfaced in her memory. What a fool she'd made of herself, prancing into his bedroom after dark, wearing a flimsy negligee. He'd rebuffed her advances, and she didn't blame him. It had been one big mistake, and she'd hated herself afterward. Not because she didn't want to be with him, but because of how she'd gone about it.

She'd tried to seduce him.

And that reminded her of how she'd seduced Wayne all those years ago.

She'd been a fish out of water then, and nothing had changed. She was no seductress. Wayne had fallen for it all those years ago, but he'd been a young man of twenty-six.

Jeff was fifty-four now, and he wouldn't fall for such antics.

Perhaps he never would have fallen for it. Wayne had been a good man and a good husband and father, but he wasn't Jeff. Jeff had an inner strength and courage that Wayne had never possessed. Maria had seen that even when Jeff insisted on rebelling against everyone and everything.

He'd paid a horrendous price for those years. Now he could have the life he'd always wanted. They could have the life they'd always wanted. Why was he fighting so hard against it?

She sighed. She'd give him more time.

She had no choice.

★ ★ ★

Thirty-Three Years Earlier

"When can I see you again?"

The words were music to Maria's ears. "Any time you want."

"You're so beautiful, my Mia," he'd said after their last kiss. "I'll pick you up after school tomorrow on the bike."

Maria hugged her pillow close. Her skin prickled, and a tickle rose between her legs. All they'd done was kiss—and they'd kissed a lot today—but she felt like she'd given more of herself to Jeff Bay in one afternoon than she'd given to Greg in the last two years. What was it about him?

He was bad news for sure. Of that she had no doubt. Bad news, that is, for everyone but her. He would never hurt her. She was one hundred percent blood positive about that. This man would never harm her in any way.

She drifted into slumber still feeling his lips upon hers.

★ ★ ★

"What the fuck do you want?"

Wayne Bay pushed past the door and stepped into Jeff's small apartment. "Grandpa's sick."

Jeff scoffed and rolled his eyes. "You think I give a rat's ass? After what he did to me?"

"You've been a jerk, Jeff. He had every right to disinherit

you."

"And that works out just great for you, the golden boy, doesn't it?" Jeff took the last drink from his can of beer and tossed the empty into the overflowing trash can in his tiny kitchen. It clattered to the floor.

"I want you to go see him."

Jeff raised his eyebrows. "Yeah? Well, I want my inheritance back. We don't always get what we want, do we?"

"If you're nice to him, show him you care, maybe he'll write you back in."

Right. Like his brother cared. Right now he got the whole enchilada. "Fat chance."

"You'll never know if you don't try."

"Don't care if the old man's got a sniffle, okay?"

"It's not just a sniffle," Wayne said. "He has pneumonia."

Jeff quelled the anxiety that rushed into his stomach. "Yeah? I hope he coughs up a lung."

"He's at Riverdale Hospital outside Grand Junction. It's really serious in a guy his age. He's not getting any younger."

Damn it! Again, he pushed the feelings of worry deep within him. "The asshole's too mean to die."

Wayne shook his head. "You'll never learn, will you?"

Jeff stood and walked Wayne to the door. "I've learned all I can from that old fool. I've learned exactly who I don't want to be when I grow up. You take your inheritance when he dies. See if I care. At least I'll go to my own grave knowing I didn't kiss some old geezer's ass to get mine."

Wayne left, still shaking his head.

Jeff opened another beer, took a drink, and then spit it in the sink. "Goddamn you, Norman Bay."

Jeff had only had one beer, and he poured the second

one down the drain. He grabbed his leather jacket and his motorcycle helmet and left the apartment, sneering.

As he rode toward the hospital, he cursed himself for going. Yet he didn't turn back. He rode all the way to the hospital and went in. Visiting hours were surely long over, but he didn't care. He checked in with the front desk and asked what room Norman Bay was in. Then he walked to the elevator and headed up.

The man looked fragile, lying in bed sleeping. Jeff didn't try to wake him up. Just stood and stared at his grandfather. Weak and old, the man had wrinkles marring his once handsome face. His gray hair, once as thick and bushy as Jeff's own, was thinning. *Sheesh, he's not even on oxygen. Can't be that bad.* But a part of his heart hurt. Those anxious feelings of fear for the old man's life crept up again. And he hated himself for them. This man had disinherited him. Practically disowned him. Had basically said, "You aren't fit to be my grandson."

Well, so be it.

In spite of himself, he was glad Grandpa looked okay. He wasn't in the ICU or anything. He'd be fine.

Of course he would.

Jeff walked quietly out of the hospital room and down the hall to the elevator.

He didn't want to go home.

So he didn't.

CHAPTER FIVE

How? How do I make myself whole again?

Even if he could afford counseling, a decent therapist in Bakersville didn't exist. He'd have to go to Denver, and that was an hour drive each way. His old truck didn't have it in her, and no way would he ask Maria to take him. Plus, he didn't want to miss the work. He was no charity case, damn it. He'd do a hard day's work to pay for his keep.

The nightmares weren't the main thing. They were coming less and less. He'd been out two years, and now they only surfaced about once a week instead of every night. That was progress, right?

He didn't have post-traumatic stress disorder. He didn't have the symptoms. No, that wasn't the problem.

He knew what the problem was.

He had to forgive *himself.* For rebelling as a young man and making such terrible decisions. For taking the fall for Max and going to prison. He'd felt he had no choice at the time after Mia's betrayal, but he'd been young and stupid. He hadn't been able to see past tomorrow. But God, he'd lived through three decades of tomorrows behind bars. So not worth it. If he'd had it to do over, he'd have just gotten over Mia and moved on with life.

"Ha!" He laughed out loud. Get over Mia and move on with life? Here he was, thirty-three years later, and he still wasn't over her.

But at least he would have been a free man.

And he had to forgive himself for not helping the innocent inmates who were brutalized almost nightly in prison.

If he could forgive his grandfather, and Wayne, and even Mia...why was he having such a difficult time granting forgiveness to himself?

He was a good man. He hadn't always been a good man, but Mia had inspired him. He'd been ready to go straight for her. If only he hadn't made that last bad decision... He'd let vengeance get in the way of what he knew was right. It had cost him everything.

He'd become a good man behind bars. He'd learned pride in his work and the satisfaction of a job well done. He'd learned empathy and the value of friendship.

He was earning his keep now, that was for sure. It felt damn good. Hard work was good for the soul. And so was honesty and a job well done.

But he wasn't whole yet.

And Maria deserved someone whole.

★ ★ ★

Thirty-Three Years Earlier

Tap.

Maria jolted in her bed.

Tap. Tap.

Her mother worked the night shift at the local convenience store. She was alone in the house except for her little sister, Meghan.

The tapping was coming from outside, against her window.

She looked at the clock. Only ten. It was early yet. Who could it be? Her neighborhood wasn't the best, but the neighbors watched out for each other. If anyone had seen anything suspicious, the cops would have been called.

She peered out her window.

"Oh!"

She stared straight into the handsome face of Jeff Bay. Her skin tingled. In the moonlight, with the silver highlighting his dark hair, he looked like a god. Already her skin tightened and the place between her legs throbbed.

She opened the window. "What are you doing here?"

He smiled his lazy grin. "I missed you."

Her breath caught. He was beautiful. "That's...nice. But it's really late, Jeff, and my little sister—"

"I won't wake her up. Can I come in just for a minute?"

"Why didn't you go to the door?"

"I didn't want to wake up your mom."

"She's at work."

"Oh. Well, no problem then. I'll go around to the door. Meet me there."

This is so not a good idea. But Maria's feet walked her to the door and her hands turned the knob and opened it. She wanted to see Jeff. She wanted to kiss him some more. She wanted to...

He grinned at her. "Nice jammies."

Oh, God. Her cheeks warmed. A cotton T-shirt a size too small and bikini underwear—what had she been thinking not pulling on some clothes before going to the door?

"Excuse me." She cleared her throat. "Go ahead and get yourself a drink in the kitchen if you want. There's soda in the fridge."

She hurried to her room and pulled on a pair of shorts and a larger T-shirt. Quickly she returned to the kitchen.

He chuckled when he saw her. "I liked the others better."

"I'm sure you did." He hadn't gotten anything, so she grabbed two cans of cola out of the fridge and handed him one. "Here you go."

"Thanks." He popped the top and took a drink. "My grandpa's in the hospital."

"Oh. I'm sorry. What's wrong?"

"Pneumonia."

"Is it serious?"

"Serious enough to put him in the hospital, I guess, but he's not in the ICU or anything. He was sleeping comfortably, as far as I could tell, when I saw him."

"That's good." She wanted to comfort him but didn't know what to say.

"We're not really that close."

Maria didn't know much about the Bays—only that their parents had died a while back and they lived with their grandfather. Both Jeff and his older brother were grown now. Still, to have the man who'd raised you sick and in the hospital had to be difficult.

"I'm sorry."

"He disinherited me."

She lurched forward. "What?"

"He wrote me out of his will. His big cattle ranch goes to my brother, Wayne. I get squat."

How awful! "Oh, Jeff..."

"Now don't give me a big pity party." He took a drink of soda. "That's not why I came over."

"Okay. Then why did you?"

He shrugged. "I...I don't know. I just wanted to see you."

She shivered. His dark gaze cut into her, stripped her of everything—her clothes, her inhibition, her good sense. "You hardly know me."

"I know. Weird, isn't it? I just met you today, but I feel like I've always known you. Like I always *want* to know you."

He felt it too? She smiled and her heartbeat quickened. She resisted the urge to go to him. "That's sweet."

He took another sip of cola and edged toward her. "Don't you feel it too?"

God, yes. "I... Well..."

He reached toward her and stroked her cheek. Fire erupted in her loins.

"You're so beautiful, Mia."

"Th-Thank you. So are you." So are you? Really? *God, I'm an idiot.*

"I want you."

She swallowed the lump that appeared in her throat. "You what?"

"Want you. I want to make love to you, Mia."

Her pulse stampeded. "You..."

"But I'll leave if you want me to. I mean, I didn't come here to...force myself on you or anything."

"Oh, I know that." And she did. In her soul she knew he'd never hurt her. How? She wasn't sure. But she knew.

"Do you...want me to go?"

Meghan was fast asleep. Mama wouldn't be home until morning. And Maria's bedroom door had a lock on it...

"I... I don't know."

"Well, you can think about it." He set the can of soda on the counter. "But I do want you. I want you like I've never wanted anything."

Her skin tingled. Her tummy fluttered. God, she wanted him too. More than she'd ever wanted Greg or anyone else. More than she wanted chocolate ice cream—her favorite—at this very moment.

She nervously took a sip of her own drink. It bubbled in her throat. The sugary aftertaste lay on her tongue, but it couldn't compare to the memory of the sweetness of Jeff's lips on hers.

Her nipples hardened under her T-shirt. She squirmed. Was she going to do this?

She knew the answer before she asked herself the question.

She would give her virginity to Jeff Bay—a man she'd known for less than twenty-four hours. The decision was crazy and impulsive and completely irresponsible.

But it was right. So right.

She knew nothing about taking a man to bed, but she didn't care. She grabbed his hand and squeezed it in her own. Without uttering a word, she led him to her bedroom.

CHAPTER SIX

Maria stood at the sink in her big country kitchen, peeling apples. Homemade applesauce for dinner tonight, along with pork chops and fried rice and onions. The combination had been one of Wayne's favorite meals—good old comfort food.

She needed a little comfort right now.

Maria was worried. She bit her upper lip as she worked with the fruit, and stopped when she tasted the metallic flavor of her own blood on her tongue. Harper said Jeff had been working every day and seemed fine, but something gnawed at Maria. Even though he resisted coming to the main house, Jeff had shared a couple of meals a week with Harper and Amber at their table since he'd come to the ranch. He hadn't been there lately.

Something was wrong.

She jumped when a throat cleared behind her.

"Ouch!" Her paring knife sliced into the palm of her hand. Blood gushed from the cut as the pain lanced into her.

"Mia!" Jeff rushed toward her. "What happened?"

Tears formed in her eyes. Just a cut, for God's sake. Yes, it hurt, but she'd had worse. Why was she crying? "I... You startled me. I cut myself."

"I'm so sorry. Here—" He took her hand and held it under the faucet.

The cool water stung at first and then soothed the smarting pain.

Jeff rummaged through drawers until he found a towel. "Let me see," he said. "Not too deep. You probably don't need stitches."

"Stitches? Oh, for goodness' sake, it's just a little cut."

"It's a pretty deep cut, Mia. What are you using for knives in here? Samurai blades?"

Mia smiled despite herself. "They're just regular forged steel knives."

Jeff wrapped the towel around her hand and applied pressure. Sparks ignited within her. For so long she'd longed for his touch. Now she was grateful to that stupid knife for giving her the opportunity. She'd have cut herself a year ago if she'd known she'd get his attention.

"Then you should be more careful. Where do you keep your bandages?"

"There are some in the powder room."

"Okay, keep holding pressure on this. I'll be right back."

He returned in a minute with a few bandages. "I'm not sure these will be big enough. Do you have any gauze and adhesive tape?"

"Jeff, don't worry about it. The bleeding has died down a lot."

"Died down doesn't mean stopped. It's a pretty deep cut. I want to get it bandaged up right."

"What do you know about bandaging a cut?"

He looked at the floor. "I worked in the infirmary for a few years in prison."

She bit her lip. "Oh." She hated talking about his time. Nausea gurgled in her stomach. The thought of him behind bars sickened her. He should have had a life...a life with her.

But she had screwed that up big time. Her own damned

fault.

"Mia, gauze and tape?"

She nodded. "There's a first aid kit upstairs. I'll go get it."

"No, you stay here. Just tell me where it is."

"It's in the hall closet, the bigger one. Top shelf, I think."

"Hold this a while longer." Jeff left the kitchen.

He returned in a few minutes with the kit. With rapt attention, he cut gauze to the right size and taped it around the palm of her hand. Then he did something totally unexpected. He raised her palm to his lips and pressed a kiss to the gauze.

Her whole body softened, nearly melted. "Oh, Jeff."

His dark gaze penetrated hers. "Mia, don't look at me like that."

She sniffed as tears wet her eyes.

He looked down at her feet. "You know, I used to dream about what our child would look like. I always imagined we'd have a little girl."

She smiled, despite her tears. "We did."

"I know that now. But when we were first together, I thought about it. I always imagined her with brown eyes, though."

"Yeah, I know. I was surprised when Angie's eyes turned green. Both you and I have brown eyes, and Wayne—" She stopped. "Anyway, Harp and Catie both have brown eyes. Angie got a recessive trait from one of us."

"She's special. I always knew our little girl would be special, if we ever had one."

"Yes. Yes, she sure is special." Maria's heart nearly broke. Again the guilt nagged at her, the pain, the life of unfulfilled love. All that could have been...if only they'd both been honest with each other back when it mattered.

She touched his cheek with her good hand and drew his gaze back to hers. "I'm so sorry, Jeff. I'm so, so sorry."

"Mia, I told you not to look at me like that."

"I don't know what you're talking about."

"That little pout. That same little pout. Oh, Mia." He crushed his mouth to hers.

The kiss was deep and passionate...

How she'd missed his kisses! The truth she'd learned all those years ago was still there in his kiss.

He didn't start slow. He pried at the seam of her lips with his tongue, and she opened for him without hesitation. Their tongues twirled and danced together, dueled, and then danced again.

His groan vibrated against her cheeks and lips, and she answered it with a groan of her own. They kissed with fervor, with passion, with an unyielding desire of three decades lost.

He nipped at her lips, bit at her, and then thrust his tongue into her mouth again and took. Yet gave at the same time, gave her something she'd never forgotten but had yearned for.

The truth of true love.

"Oh, Jeff," she moaned into his lips.

"Kiss me, Mia," he said against her skin. "Kiss me."

"Always."

He cupped her cheeks as he kissed her again. She let her hands wander to his broad shoulders, still hard and firm as she remembered. She trailed downward. His nipples were hard against the soft fabric of his work shirt. She flicked over one with her fingernail. He groaned in her mouth.

Yes, yes, he used to love that. She remembered every inch of his body. Every inch she had discovered that wonderful night in her bedroom. Not once had she forgotten him. Not one day had she gone without thinking of him during all those years they'd spent apart.

She poured thirty years of passion into that kiss. Thirty years of love.

Yet still he broke away, panting.

His eyes were misty, troubled, filled with sorrow and regret.

"I'm sorry, Mia. I can't."

★ ★ ★

Thirty-Three Years Earlier

Maria clicked the lock on her door, sat down on her bed, and motioned for Jeff to join her.

"I don't really know what I'm doing," she said, shivering. She rubbed her arms to warm them. "I've never..."

"Shh." He traced her lips with his finger. "It's okay. I don't care about any of that. I just want you."

"I want you too."

He kissed her mouth gently, sweetly. "If you want to stop, you just tell me. I'll never do anything you don't want me to do."

She nodded. Right now she wanted everything, and she wanted it with him. If she only had this one night, she could live on it the rest of her life, she was sure. He was that special, that important.

Clarity dawned as though the truth had always existed. This was why she'd never slept with Greg, even those few nights when she was so turned on from making out she'd had to squeeze her legs shut. Even then, it had never felt right.

This felt right.

"I want this," she said. "Show me what to do, Jeff."

He kissed her again, an innocent kiss. He slowly inched the T-shirt up, exposing her bare skin and leaving blazes in his wake. He left her lips for a moment to pull the shirt over her head.

"Oh, God, Mia, you're so beautiful."

He bent down and kissed one taut nipple. She shuddered. How could anything feel as good as his mouth on her breast? The act of sex itself couldn't possibly be any better than this one moment.

She savored it, froze it in her memory, the sensation of his lips on her nipple. He found the other with his fingers and lightly flicked them over it. More sparks flew to her belly and landed between her legs. Oh, the sensation, the sweet surrender to his lips. When he darted his tongue out and touched the nipple, she flew. Then he closed his lips around the hard peak and sucked.

Her clit throbbed. Each movement he made, each sensation he uncovered in her, took her to a higher place. She never wanted to come down again.

Gently he laid her on the bed and eased her shorts off. Now nothing stood between her private parts and him except her bikini undies.

She shuddered as he took off his shirt. His skin was so creamy, so beautiful, and his chest so perfectly sculpted. Of its own accord, her hand reached out and her fingers touched his nipple. He quivered beneath her touch. Would it feel as good to him as it did to her if she put her mouth there? She'd have to find out.

He leaned down and kissed her nipple again, then the other one. He cupped her breasts and squeezed them, and then trailed tiny kisses all over her chest and abdomen, down to where her panties covered her. He eased her panties over her thighs. She kicked them off.

"So beautiful," he said again. He parted her legs.

She closed her eyes. She wasn't embarrassed. Not at all, which surprised her. She trusted him. Welcomed his touch and his gaze.

He spread her legs wide. One finger trailed over her folds. She quivered. Dear God, his touch set her aflame!

"So pretty. And so wet, my Mia. For me."

Wet? She must be sopping. She closed her eyes and sighed. Her heart did little flip-flops, and flutters filled her tummy. When something soft and wet touched her, her eyes flew open.

His tongue. He was licking her down there. And oh, how good it felt. Unimaginably and indescribably good.

"Mmm, you taste good, Mia," he said against her mound. "So good." He lapped at her, tonguing her clit, and then swiping all the way up and down her opening. Then a finger breached her.

It was tight, but it felt amazing, as if she'd been empty and was only now beginning to be filled. Slowly he moved it in and out of her. She gasped when he inserted another finger, but soon she got used to the invasion. Again he moved them slowly, in and out.

"This will get you used to having something in there," he said. "How does it feel?"

She sighed, sinking into her comforter. "It feels wonderful, Jeff. Wonderful."

Out of nowhere, she wanted to put her mouth to him. Greg had begged her to do that, but the thought had disgusted her. Now, she wanted it more than anything. She wanted to do it...for Jeff.

Later, though. For now, she closed her eyes and reveled in what he was doing to her. He tantalized her, stroked her, kissed her, pulled at her with his lips and teeth, all the while thrusting his long thick fingers in and out of her channel.

His fingers inside her felt so good she thought she might burst... Oh, stop, stop, he had to stop...and then a rainbow exploded inside her body.

Her voice came from somewhere else. "Jeff, Jeff, that feels so good. Oh, Jeff!"

"Yeah, beautiful, baby. Beautiful. So sweet, my Mia."

When she stopped convulsing, she opened her eyes and met his smoky gaze. She opened her mouth, but no words emerged. The comforter hugged her like a fluffy cloud, and nirvana cloaked her.

"You're beautiful when you come," Jeff said.

Her insides quivered. So that was a climax. How was it possible to feel so good? So right? She could die right now and know she'd experienced true pleasure.

He reached for her hand and led it to the hardness under his jeans. "Touch me, Mia. Please."

Forcing herself from her rapture, she rubbed her hand over the hard spot, unsure what to do. She wanted to please him, needed to please him. "Show me, Jeff. Show me how to make you feel that good."

He smiled, unzipped his jeans, and slid them over his hips along with his briefs. His erection sprang forward from a patch of black curls. It was regal, it was beautiful...it was so big!

Could she go through with this? Yes, because she wanted

to, wanted more than anything in the world for him to be inside her body—to be a part of her.

Jeff smiled at her and whispered again, "Touch me." He took her hand and led it to his erection. It was so hard yet silky at the same time. Its warmth radiated into her hand and up her arm.

"Ah, yes," he said. "That feels good, Mia." He moved her hand up and down his shaft, showing her how to stroke him. "Like that, baby. Just like that."

Mia slid her fist over Jeff's cock in wonder. How such a small movement on her part could make him feel so good amazed her. And turned her on.

"Jeff," she said shyly.

His eyes were closed. "Yes?" he said in a voice that seemed lower than normal.

"I want... I want..."

"What? What do you want?"

"I want to put my mouth on you."

"Oh my God," he groaned.

"Show me how."

"Just do whatever you want. I'll love it. I promise."

She lowered her head and darted her tongue out to taste his cock head. It was salty, and a drop of fluid emerged. She licked it up. Salty again.

He quivered. "God, Mia. God damn."

She swirled her tongue around the salty head again, and then again. Then she took it into her mouth and sucked gently.

His whole body tensed. "God, God, Mia."

She loved making him groan, making him quiver. She returned to her task and took more of him into her mouth. He was so huge, but she wanted so badly to please him. Wanted to make him feel as good as he'd made her feel.

And she would.

She sucked him as far as she could into her mouth, stopping when he touched the back of her throat. She let go before she gagged.

She tried again. Did better this time.

All the while he moaned and groaned, telling her how beautiful she was, how good she was making him feel.

Suddenly he jerked away. His dick slid from her mouth.

Her heart slammed against her chest. "What? Did I do something wrong?"

"God, no. You did something very right. But I don't want it to be over yet. I want to make love to you."

"You mean...?"

"Yeah. If you keep doing that I'm going to come, and I don't want to come in your mouth. Well, I do, but not tonight. Tonight I want to come inside you."

Oh, she wanted it too. Already she was gearing up for another orgasm. The tickle between her legs had returned, and moisture settled on her inner thighs.

"Yes, Jeff. I want that too."

"You are so beautiful." He traced her cheekbone with his index finger. "Will I be your first?"

Her cheeks warmed—from his touch or from his question, she wasn't sure. "Yes, Jeff."

"Mia, I want to be your first and only." He shook his head, his lips trembling. "I can't believe I'm saying it right now, but God, that's what I want."

Her first. Yes, she was ready. She wanted him so much. So much more than she'd ever desired Greg or anyone else. "Please, Jeff," she said, "make love to me."

He reached between her legs. "You're wet again, Mia. So wet for me."

Yes, she was. She was so ready for him. Ready for this, with this man and no other.

But he pulled away.

"Jeff?"

"Just need to get the condom out of my wallet."

"Oh." Of course. Contraception. Was she truly so turned on that she was willing to risk pregnancy? Thank God Jeff had the sense to remember.

"Aw, shit." He threw his jeans down.

"What?"

"It's gone. I forgot. I gave it to my friend Trey yesterday. God damn it!"

Maria nearly broke into tears. She was ready. So ready. "Can't you just pull out?"

"That's so hard, baby. You don't even know."

"Please?"

He came back to her, lay down next to her. "It's not a hundred percent effective. Are you willing to take that risk?"

Her pulse thundered in her neck. "Nothing is one hundred percent effective, is it?"

He smiled. "No. The only thing that's a hundred percent effective is for me to leave right now."

"Are you willing to do that?" *Please say no. Please say no.*

"I would if you asked me to."

She warmed all over. Such a gentleman. "That's so kind of you, Jeff, but I'm not asking. Please, I trust you. Pull out. You can do it."

He closed his eyes and let out a groan. "God, Mia..."

"Please..."

He stroked her clit, making her even wetter, and then he dipped first one finger and then two into her, teasing her channel as he'd done before.

"It might hurt, but only for a little while." He looked into her eyes, his dark gaze smoldering. "I'll ask you one more time. Are you sure about this?"

Her entire body warmed, and the truth hit her like a lightning bolt. She was more sure than she was that the sun would rise tomorrow. "Yes, I'm sure. Very sure."

He moved on top of her and nudged at her entrance with his erection. "God, Mia, God, I can't wait any longer." He thrust inside her.

"Oh!" She sucked in a breath. Pain, yes, but not what she'd expected. Just a little, then she felt only full.

He stayed still, but his body shuddered. She could tell he wanted to move, wanted to thrust. He was waiting for her to get used to his invasion.

"Are you okay?" he whispered against her neck.

She bit her lip. "Yes. I'm fine. It didn't hurt that much."

"Good. I want you to feel good. I'll try to make this good for you."

"It's already good for me, Jeff. I promise." She'd never spoken truer words.

His perspiration spilled onto her neck and face. He still hesitated.

"Please, I promise." She wiped the moisture from his forehead with her hand. "It's okay. I'm okay."

"God," he groaned. He pulled out and then thrust back in.

She sucked in another breath, but the pain wasn't nearly as intense. In fact, it really wasn't pain at all.

He pulled out and pushed in again, and then again. And gradually the sensations turned from uncomfortable to wonderful. His cock brushed her clit each time he thrust into her, and her channel began to throb.

Yes, this was what it was about, how it was supposed to be. Not pain, but pleasure. Pure raw pleasure, to have a man inside her. A man she wanted there.

She moaned his name, urged him to thrust faster, harder. And with each plunge of his cock into her core, her pleasure increased, until the now familiar spasms that started inside her vagina threaded outward to her belly, her legs, upward to her heart, and down to the tips of her toes.

Nothing had ever felt so good, and nothing, she was sure, would ever feel so good again.

He thrust and he thrust, moaning her name, telling her how beautiful she was, how good she made him feel.

"God, Mia. God, yes. Yes, yes."

As his thrusts increased in speed and pressure, she began the ascent to the precipice again, and soon the sensations flooded her once more—raw pleasure, pure nirvana.

"That's right, baby. Come for me. Come for me again." He pushed inside her one last time and held his cock there against the walls of her convulsing channel, deep inside her as he breathed out heavily.

"I'm coming, Mia. Oh, God, I'm coming."

Those words fortified her heart and soul. He was coming. For her. She had made him feel this good. Her. Simple Maria Gomez from the other side of the tracks. She had brought Jeff Bay to his knees.

She whimpered when he pulled out of her and groaned, holding his cock. In the dark, she couldn't see, but his trembling made it clear what was happening. He was ejaculating...all over her bed. She hadn't thought of that...

When his breathing slowed to nearly normal, he lay next to her. "I'm sorry. About the mess."

"It's okay."

He grabbed a tissue off her nightstand and wiped up the wetness. Then he gathered her in his arms and pulled her close.

"Mia, that was amazing."

She nodded, couldn't speak.

"Did you like it?"

Did she like it? Words couldn't express how much this had meant to her. If only they could, she would tell him exactly what she meant. But she said only, "Yes."

"Good." He kissed her forehead and smiled. "I'm glad."

She wanted to ask him where they'd go from here. Was he her boyfriend now? She wouldn't presume anything. Perhaps he'd only wanted the sex, and she could live with that if she had to. This experience had been worth it. But oh, she hoped he wanted more. She hoped this was the first of many miracles between them.

She opened her mouth, but she had no idea what to say.

It didn't matter anyway.

The knock on the door would have silenced her.

CHAPTER SEVEN

Maria's heart dropped to her belly. "Why, Jeff? Why can't you? I know you want me. You know I want you. I never stopped loving you. Never, no matter how my decisions may have looked in the past."

"I know." Jeff's Adam's apple bobbed in his neck. "You did it for Angie."

"That's right."

"You didn't believe in me."

So he was back to this again. "I'm sorry. I felt I had no choice at the time." What more could she say? She'd said it all time and again.

"If you had believed in me..."

Anger rose within her. Maria tried to tamp it down, but the words came out anyway. "Oh, stop it. You know I had no choice. I thought you were going to prison, and it turns out I was right." When he opened his mouth to speak, she held up a hand to quiet him. "No, I didn't think you were a killer, Jeff. I never thought that. But the evidence was there, and the cops needed a scapegoat."

"It doesn't matter anymore." Jeff sighed. "I just can't, Mia, and that's that."

She sniffed, her eyes watering. "You're never going to forgive me, are you?"

Jeff shook his head. "It's not as simple as you might think."

She opened her heart and reached for him. "Jeff, my love, I know you've been through hell. I can't even begin to imagine all you've experienced while I've been here on the ranch with your daughter and her siblings. I've had a wonderful life, even without being in love, and you've suffered. I wish I could change it. I truly do. I'd give up everything if I could give you your life back. I would."

His dark eyes misted. He looked away. "I know you would, Mia."

She widened her eyes, shocked. "You know? You believe me?"

"Yes, I do."

"Oh, Jeff." She fell against his hard chest. "Thank you for that. Thank you."

His arms went around her, tightened, and for a moment, as she was cocooned in his embrace, everything was right. Until he pulled away.

"It doesn't change anything, Mia."

She looked up into his handsome face tight with tension. His beautiful eyes were sunken and sad.

"What can I do, Jeff? What can I do to change things between us? We both deserve happiness after all we've been through, you most of all. I want to make you happy. That's what I want most in the world."

"I know, Mia. I know."

"Why won't you let me?"

He sucked in a long breath and let it out slowly. He backed away. "I just can't."

★ ★ ★

Thirty-Three Years Earlier

"Shh," Maria said to Jeff. "Don't say a word."

Jeff nodded.

Maria walked to the door, her heart skittering. "Who is it?"

"It's me," her sister, Meghan, said. "Who else would it be?"

Maria gathered her courage. "What do you want? Why aren't you asleep?"

"I heard noises. Can I sleep with you?"

Maria drew in a deep breath. Meghan was only eleven and prone to nightmares since their father had died a year ago. Often she crawled in bed with Maria when she couldn't sleep. Clearly that couldn't happen tonight.

What was she going to do?

"Just a minute, Meghan." Quickly she pulled on her T-shirt and undies and wrapped a robe around her shoulders.

"Stay here," she mouthed to Jeff.

She unlocked the door, went into the hallway, and shut her door behind her. "It's okay, honey. Did you have another bad dream?"

"No. I told you. I heard noises."

"What kind of noises?"

"Squeaking or something. And some voices."

"Oh?" How could she have been so stupid as to make love in her bedroom with Meghan in the other room? What had she been thinking?

Right. She knew exactly what she'd been thinking. The next world war wouldn't have stopped her from sleeping with

Jeff. She'd wanted it that much, felt it was that right.

It *had* been.

"Okay, honey. Let's have a look around." She took Meghan's hand and led her through the house on the ritual that had become habit when Meghan woke. They turned on the lights in each room and checked behind everything to put the younger girl at ease.

"See?" Maria said. "No one's here except you and me. Let's get you back to bed."

"But we didn't check your room."

A chill crept up Maria's neck. Jeff was in her room, probably still naked in her bed. "I was just in there, honey. My room is fine."

"But we always check all the rooms," Meghan persisted.

"Honey, come on. I'm so tired." Maria feigned a yawn. "Let's just get you back to bed."

"Please? I'll never get back to sleep."

Before Maria could stop her, Meghan turned the doorknob, opened the door to Maria's room, and walked in.

Maria caught her breath. How would she explain this? Her skin prickled with nerves as she followed her sister into her room.

The bed was mussed. And the window wide open. An autumn breeze drifted into the room. Thank God they lived in a small ranch house.

She took a deep breath and started the ritual. "See? Nothing here either."

"Why's your window open? That's not safe."

Maria shut it quickly. "I was warm a little earlier. I must have fallen asleep before I remembered to shut it."

That seemed to appease Meghan.

"Let's get you back to bed now."

Thankfully, Meghan didn't beg to sleep with Maria. She couldn't bear the thought of lying in her bed, remembering her wonderful time with Jeff...with her little sister next to her. She tucked Meghan back into bed, gave her a quick kiss on the forehead, and went back to her room.

She closed her bedroom door, inhaled deeply, and sat down on the bed. It was still warm. She smiled. She would never forget this night.

A tap on the window startled her.

She jumped up to see Jeff's nose pressed against the window. She quickly opened it.

"What'd you shut it for?" he asked.

"Sorry. I didn't know you were coming back."

"I wouldn't leave you without saying good-bye." He climbed in the window.

"Shh." She smiled. Of course he wouldn't leave her. She wished he could stay with her and hold her all night, but that was impossible.

As if reading her mind, he said, "Can I stay?" His beautiful lips were curved in a lazy grin.

"I so wish you could, Jeff. But Meghan's awake now, and I know she'd hear us."

"Hmm. We'll have to find a better place then. My apartment next time?"

Her heart nearly leaped out of her chest. Next time! A next time would happen. She smiled.

He continued, "You could spend the night there, no problem."

Reality came down hard and hit her in the gut. "Well, no, I couldn't. My mom works nights, and I have to stay with

Meghan."

"Oh."

His gorgeous lips turned downward. He looked hurt. Well, heck, she wasn't too crazy about the situation either, but what could she do?

"Tomorrow afternoon then. I'll pick you up after school." He grinned. "Unless you want to skip again."

Skip? With only two weeks left, why not? But she did still have finals to think about, even though her grades were inconsequential at this point. At her core, Maria Gomez was a good girl—a good girl who didn't cut school, even for the man of her dreams.

"I can't cut again. I still have to graduate."

He winked. "Okay. For this time anyway. I'll pick you up after school on my bike."

She smiled, her whole body warming. "I'll be waiting."

He trailed a finger down her cheek and then lowered his lips to hers.

The kiss was slow and gentle this time. A kiss not of passion, not of urgency, but of completion and understanding.

A kiss of love.

Was it possible to fall in love in a day? Who knew? Maria had said "I love you" to Greg Black once, when he'd said it to her—when he was trying to get her to go further, of course— but she'd never felt the wholeness and completeness that she felt with Jeff Bay. The desire and the need. So what did time have to do with it?

She was in love for the first time in her life, with Jeff Bay, a bad boy, but such a sweet, wonderful man.

All those others were wrong about Jeff. They had to be. Any man who could kiss like that and make love to a woman so tenderly and completely her very first time was a wonderful man. A perfect man.

When he lifted his mouth from hers, she pressed her lips together. Otherwise, she was afraid she'd blurt out, "I love you."

His dark gaze penetrated hers. He was so handsome, and even in the darkness his eyes glittered.

"I'll see you tomorrow then, Mia."

"Yes," she whispered, "tomorrow."

In a flash, he climbed back out the window and was gone.

Maria drifted into her bed once more.

And still, it was warm.

CHAPTER EIGHT

"Hi there, Angie."

Jeff stood at the door of his home on Cha Cha Ranch and regarded his daughter's beautiful face. Her dark hair was tied in twin ponytails behind each ear. He longed to reach out and grab her, never let her go. He'd seen a few old photos. She'd been a gorgeous little girl, the pride of his brother's eye. He gulped. No sense resenting his dead brother. The situation was what it was.

"Sorry to barge in like this," Angie said.

"Not a problem." Jeff held the door open. "This used to be your home, after all."

"Yeah, every now and then I miss the old place." She shook her head. "No, I'll be honest. I really don't miss it. I didn't...like myself very much during the time I lived here."

"Why do you say that?"

"Oh, you know how spoiled I was. My fa— Er, uncle. God." She let out a sigh. "That doesn't sound right either."

"You were Wayne's favorite. I know. Your mother has told me all the stories." He attempted a smile. "I guess I should be grateful to my brother for doting on you, for giving you everything you deserved."

A tear formed in the corner of Angie's right eye.

"What's wrong?" Jeff asked.

"It's just...I loved my father...I..."

"It's okay for you to call him your father, Angie. He was

your father in every way that counted. I just wish I could have been the one to... Oh, well. That's neither here nor there."

"The thing is I wasn't a very good person. Before."

"Before what?"

"Before I met Rafe. I was spoiled rotten, and...well, according to my mother, it was my father who spoiled me. And she let him, because she felt so guilty about deceiving him that I was his. She didn't have the heart to tell him to stop it."

"Angie, it's—"

"Please—" She held up a hand. "Let me finish."

Jeff nodded.

"Harper and Catie weren't like me. They weren't spoiled rotten. They were good kids, hard workers. I mean, you can see that now."

"Yes, they're both great people."

"And I wasn't...not for a long time."

"But you are now, Angie, and that's all that matters."

"I've done a lot of things in my life that I'm not very proud of."

Jeff laughed. He couldn't help it. "You are preaching to the choir, honey. Believe me, no matter how spoiled rotten you were, anything rotten you did fits on the head of a pin compared to what I've done."

"I didn't mean—"

"I know you didn't. It's okay if you weren't perfect. It's even okay if you were a spoiled brat. Accept your past and move on."

She sniffed. "Can you?"

Her question hit his gut like a bowling ball. God, he wished he could. There was so much his innocent daughter didn't know about him.

"Are you going to answer me?"

Jeff bit his lip. "I don't really know what to say."

"Mama... She loves you, I think," Angie said. "I mean, she hasn't told me, but the way she looks at you... She never looked at Daddy... I'm sorry. I did it again." She rubbed her forehead.

"I said it's okay, Angie."

"They weren't in love. They admitted it. And I think it's sad to go through life without love, don't you?"

Jeff nodded, trying not to get misty.

"I mean, what Rafe and I have—Mama and Daddy never had that. And I think that's really sad. They deserved it, and Daddy will never have it now."

Jeff nodded again. "I know. I'm sorry about that."

Angie sniffed. "But Mama can, Jeff. You and Mama can."

Could they? Jeff wasn't sure. He was no longer a whole man. "I'm not the man I was thirty-some-odd years ago, Angie. I'm not the man your mother fell in love with."

"But you're still Jeff Bay. She fell in love with Jeff Bay. Oh!" She clutched at her belly.

Jeff reached for her. "What is it, sweetheart?"

"It's...oh, it can't be. A contraction? I'm not due for three weeks. Although I was early myself—" She shook her head. "No, I wasn't, after all. That's the story Mama always told to cover up my paternity. I was actually a few days late— Oh!"

"Angie?"

"Oh, God. I think my water just broke. My belly's been giving me fits for the last several hours. It felt like indigestion, but—oh my God—this isn't indigestion."

Jeff looked at Angie's midsection. Sure enough, her shorts were drenched, and clear fluid trickled down her legs.

Jeff didn't know much about births, but he did know that once the water broke, the baby was coming.

"Oh, Jesus, okay." He looked around. "Let's get you into the spare bedroom. You can lie down and I'll call the doctor."

"I want Rafe."

"Of course. I'll call him."

"But he's in Grand Junction, meeting with the foreman at Bay Crossing. He... He didn't want to go. Didn't want to leave me. I insisted, said I was fine. Oh my God, what was I thinking?"

"You were thinking you were fine, and you are."

"He can't miss the birth of our first child."

"He may not. Labor can go on for a while, can't it? He's only a few hours away."

That seemed to calm her down. "Yes, yes. He'll get here."

"Of course he will." Jeff wished he were as sure as his voice sounded. He helped Angie to the spare bedroom. He quickly spread a clean cotton sheet over the bed—just in case—and gently laid her down.

"Call Rafe, please?"

"Of course, but I need to call the doctor first."

"Oh!" She clutched her belly. "God, another one already?"

Crap. Jeff looked at his watch. It had been what—two minutes since the last one? That couldn't be good. Weren't they supposed to start at ten minutes apart?

"Call Rafe," she said again.

"The doctor, Angie. Where's your phone?"

"In my purse, in the living room."

Jeff ran to the living room and retrieved the purse. He fished for her cell phone, and when he found it, browsed through the contacts list. There, Dr. Feinstein. He placed the call.

"Dr. Feinstein's answering service."

Shit. Really? "Hello. I'm the fa—uncle of one of Dr. Feinstein's patients, Angelina Grayhawk. She's gone into labor and we're an hour away from Denver, outside Bakersville."

"How far apart are her contractions, sir?"

"About two or three minutes."

"And has her water broken?"

"Yes, it has."

"We'll page Dr. Feinstein. He's on call. In the meantime, get her to Denver right away."

Angie screamed from the other room. "I have to push."

"I don't have a car. But I'll call her mother. She can... Shit, she's in Denver already for the day. My nephew is out on the ranch, I'll have to find him."

"What about you, sir?"

"I don't have a car."

"Just get her to the hospital in Denver as soon as you can."

"She's saying she needs to push."

"Push? Oh goodness, there may not be time to get her to the hospital."

"What do you mean? This is her first baby, for God's sake."

"It's a myth that first babies are always slow. Sometimes they come quickly. When that baby is ready to come, he's going to come, and there's nothing you or I can do about it. Call 9-1-1 and get an ambulance on the way. In the meantime, do what you can to keep her comfortable. Once I get hold of Dr. Feinstein, he'll call you. May I give him the number you called on?"

"Of course. It's Angie's phone."

"He'll call as soon as he can. Now dial 9-1-1 and get that ambulance moving."

"Yes, yes, of course." Jeff had no idea what he was doing. But he had to be strong. His little girl needed him. Her husband wasn't here. Her doctor wasn't here. His brother— the only father she'd ever known—wasn't here. He—Jeff—was all she had.

He would not fail her.

Quickly he dialed 9-1-1. "Hello? This is Jeff Bay. My daughter is in labor. Her water has broken and her contractions are two minutes apart."

"Oh!" Angie screamed in the background.

Jeff's nerves shattered. God, what was he going to do?

"Sir?" the operator on the line said.

"Yes, I'm here."

"Where are you?"

"The Bay Ranch, Cha Cha, outside Bakersville. I don't have a car or I'd drive her to Denver. Her doctor's answering service said to call for an ambulance. Shit! I don't know what to do."

"Is this her first baby, sir?"

"Yes. I'm scared shitless here."

"You'll probably be fine. First babies usually come slowly."

"That's not what the doc's office said."

"Sir, I'm dispatching the ambulance. Everything will be fine."

"Easy for you to say." He clicked off the phone.

"Have you called Rafe yet?" Angie screamed from the other room.

God! What a terrible father he was. He'd left her alone in that guest room, and he hadn't called the person she wanted most in the world—her husband.

He stumbled back into the guest room and scanned Angie's phone for Rafe's number. "I'm calling him now, sweetheart."

No answer. Damn! He had to stop himself from throwing the phone at the wall.

"I'm sorry, honey, he's not answering."

"He's"—Angie let out a deep breath—"probably out working on the ranch. Probably can't hear the phone."

"Damn it all to hell."

He redialed and left a voice mail. Hopefully he didn't sound too completely useless. He wanted Rafe to know his wife was in good hands.

But was she? He didn't know squat about pregnant women or delivering babies. Working in the infirmary of a prison that housed only males certainly hadn't prepared him for this. But he had to be there for his daughter.

"He'll be on his way as soon as he can," he soothed his daughter. "I'm sure of it."

"Yes, yes," she panted. "I know he will be. He wouldn't want to miss"—more pants—"any of this."

"Are you okay, honey? Can I get you anything?"

"How about some drugs? Or just knock me unconscious with a freaking mallet. I don't righteously care at this point."

"God, I'm sorry. Is the pain that bad?"

"Well, it's like the world's worst case of gas pain and menstrual cramps, and then multiply it by a hundred or so."

Jeff paced along the floor by the foot of the bed. What to do?

In a flash, he thought of Maria giving birth to Angie. The pain she must have borne to bring their daughter into the world. He should have been there. Instead, his brother had been. A sense of gratitude overwhelmed him. Maria hadn't been alone. Wayne had been there for her.

Thank you. He mouthed the words to his dead brother. *Thank you for being there when I couldn't be.*

And the last tiny shred of resentment toward Wayne melted away.

★ ★ ★

Thirty-Three Years Earlier

"I hear you rode off on some delinquent's bike."

Maria looked up from the book she was reading to face Greg Black, his brown eyes angry. "Where'd you hear that?"

"From everyone. Are you trying to make a fool out of me, Maria?"

"No, of course not." She didn't want to hurt Greg. He wasn't "the one," but she still cared about him. But after what she'd shared with Jeff, she had to end things with Greg— something she should have done a while ago.

"Don't think I've forgotten that you're eighteen now. Your old excuses aren't holding up anymore. When are we going to go all the way?"

Never. And Maria was so glad she hadn't succumbed to Greg before now. She felt bad about breaking up, but her emotion lessened after that comment. Everything was about sex with him. Well, that definitely wasn't going to happen. They were over. They had been since the moment Jeff Bay met her gaze that first day.

"Greg, we need to talk."

"Putting me off again, are you?" He shook his head.

"No." Maria cleared her throat. "I mean yes. I...think it's time to break up."

He shook his head again, his eyes wide. "Are you serious? You put me off for a year, and now you're ending things? You're a fucking tease, Maria."

"You don't understand—"

"You're damned right I don't. I gave up a lot of ass, waiting for you. I could have been screwing the whole cheerleading squad!"

"Well, now you're free to do so." Maria stood from the bench outside the school. "Go for it."

Greg yanked on her arm. "We're doing it, you little bitch."

Her stomach dropped as icy fear boiled in her. They were right outside the school. Granted, it was after hours and very few people were around. She'd been waiting for Shelley to pick her up after a club meeting. But they were out in the open. Surely he couldn't think...

"Let go of me. I'm sorry if I hurt you, but I need to break up with you, Greg."

His angry gaze met hers. He held on to her arm for a few more seconds and then dropped it. "You're not worth it."

Words she'd heard more than once from various sources—although they were usually hurtful, she was happy to be hearing them now.

He turned and walked away.

★ ★ ★

"We're gonna rob your old man," Max said, his hazel

eyes cold.

"Say what?" Jeff jerked his neck around so hard it hurt.

"Did I stutter? We're gonna rob Grandpa Norman. You always say the old coot hates banks and keeps most of his wealth in a safe in the house."

"Yeah, but—"

"And you're always saying how you got cheated out of your inheritance by your grandpa and your sainted brother. We're your buddies. We're gonna help you out. We're gonna get your share back for you, and then, of course, you'll split it with us."

"No way," Jeff said. "I'm having no part of that. It's one thing to hold up a damned liquor store. No fucking way am I going to hold up my own family."

"What the hell have they ever done for you?"

Good point. Those two fuckers would no doubt rather see Jeff dead. Maybe Max was onto something. Of course, Norman was in the hospital. Which actually might make things a little easier. He'd only have to get the combinations—but how?—and then they could get in and out while Wayne was either out of the house or asleep. Asleep might be better. Jeff could slip him a sedative or something. Or get him drunk and wait until he passed out.

Of course, the golden boy didn't imbibe much.

He'd find a way. One way or another, Jeff would get what he was entitled to, and Golden Boy would get what he deserved.

He cleared his throat. "What's the plan, then?"

"We'll be masked, of course. No sense you getting into trouble if they see it's you. All we need you to do is get us into the house and get us the combinations to all your grandfather's safes."

"I don't know. How would I get those combos? They sure as hell wouldn't give them to me."

"Take big brother out for a drink and slip him a little something so he starts talking."

"I'm not even sure Wayne knows." Jeff knew that was a lie as soon as it left his mouth. Of course Wayne knew. Norman trusted him with everything. But drug his brother? Could he do that?

Yeah, he could. What the fuck? The stuff was rightfully his anyway. He was sick to death of being cheated. It would stop, as of now.

Wayne no doubt knew the combinations. Grandpa trusted Pretty Boy with everything. But no way would Wayne divulge that information to the likes of his little brother. Probably the only way to get the combinations was to scare the shit out of Wayne.

That he could do. All he needed was a little ketamine, which he could get from the local vet. His assistant had been known to take a bribe.

"I'll get them tonight." And then he washed Max and robbing Grandpa from his mind.

He had an all-day ride with Mia to get to.

CHAPTER NINE

"I want Rafe," Angie sobbed.

"I know, honey. He's coming as fast as he can. You just stay strong now, and I'm going to take good care of you."

She winced and leaned forward. "God, it hurts!"

"I know, darlin'. Just hold on. I'm here and I won't let anything happen."

"This is crazy! I'm no granola girl. I want to be in a hospital with— Oh!" She doubled over, huffing. "Drugs, damn it! I wouldn't have a root canal without drugs. Why would I try to push a human being out of my body without drugs?"

What to do? She was three weeks early, and this was her first baby. "There's all kinds of time, Angie. You don't need to worry. You're not going to have this baby for many hours yet. Rafe will get here. The ambulance will get here. You'll get to the hospital. There's no need to worry."

"I need to push, damn it!"

"It's just an urge. It'll pass."

"Pass? Are you freaking serious? What the hell do you know about it? Passed any football-sized kidney stones lately?"

What could he say to her? His daughter. His little girl. He should know her better, should have been here for her long before now.

Water under the bridge, Jeff. He couldn't think about that right now. Right now Angie was in labor, and she needed him to stay calm and help her until Rafe and the ambulance arrived. He had to take care of her. Damn it, he *would* take care of her. He was her father and he would not let her down. Why hadn't he paid more attention growing up on the ranch? He'd seen calves being born, foals...

"Breathe, sweetie. Did you take those birthing classes? Did they teach you to breathe through your contractions or something like that?"

"Yes, yes, I took those stupid-ass classes. They gave me a biology lesson about stuff I already knew and— Oh, shit!"

Angie leaned over the side of the bed and heaved.

"Honey? You okay?"

She swiped her hand across her mouth. "Do I look okay to you? I just threw up. Or at least I wanted to. Nothing came up." Her forehead was slick with perspiration, and the dark hairs that had come loose from her ponytails stuck to her face.

"I'm sure that's very normal. I'll get you a basin or something, okay?"

"No!" she shrieked.

He turned back, his eyebrows lifted. "Angie?"

"Don't leave me, Daddy. Please."

Daddy.

The word melted into his heart like warm honey. He wished he could lie down and let the sweet melody of it spread through him for hours.

But now was not the time to get caught up in emotion. His little girl needed him.

"Please, honey, I'm just going to the other room. I want to get you a basin and some water. A cold rag for your head. Okay?"

She nodded, her lips trembling.

He gathered every bit of his strength to leave her. He stumbled out of the room and ran to the kitchen, knocking over a standing plant and an empty glass off the sofa table at the head of the stairs. *God damn it!* Water. Ice. Crushed ice? Was that it? Some episode of a television show he'd seen during rec hour in prison... Was it *ER*? Ice chips for women in labor. Yeah, that sounded right.

Plus a basin for her nausea. And a cool rag for her forehead. The poor thing was sweating bullets.

"Daddy!" she cried.

Music to his ears. "I'm coming, darlin'."

"Daddy, I have to push."

"Can't you hold off? The ambulance is sure to be here, and—"

"Please," she said. "I have to push."

Damn! What could he do? He could fire up his iPad and search the Internet for emergency births...but he didn't want to leave her.

He'd already called 9-1-1 and the doctor. Who else?

The local doctor, of course. Larson was his name. Would he be on Angie's phone? Yes! He called the number. Got voice mail—Doc was in Denver at a seminar for two days.

God damn it! And he called himself a doctor? Who else? The vet?

Heck, yeah. She might have a clue. She delivered calves and foals—how much different could it be? Plus this child was sort of related to her. She was married to Dallas McCray, the brother of Chad McCray, who was Angie's sister, Catie's, husband. He grabbed his cell phone out of his pocket and dialed Annie McCray.

"Yeah, this is Annie," she said.

"Annie, thank God. It's Jeff Bay over at Cha Cha. Angie's here and she's gone into labor. Doc Larson is in Denver for a seminar. I've called an ambulance, but God knows when they'll get out here. Rafe's on the western slope and is on his way." Jeff hoped he was, anyway. He would be when he got Jeff's voicemail. "Can you possibly help?"

"Calm down. It's going to be all right. How far apart are her contractions?"

"Just a few minutes. And she says she wants to push. Her water broke an hour ago."

"Okay. I'm on my way. It'll take me about ten minutes to get up there. In the meantime, get her undressed from the waist down. If she wants to push, she's going to be having that baby no matter how inconvenient it is for everyone else. That's Angie's way, isn't it?"

Jeff had to chuckle. He hadn't known his daughter long, but he knew that about her. When she set her mind to something, she got what she wanted. And right now, she seemed to want to have this baby.

"She can't have a baby in her clothes, so get her undressed and lying down on a clean surface."

"She's on my guest bed. I put clean sheets over the covers. What about boiling water?"

"You watch too much TV. Don't leave her to go boil water. Get her to lie on her side. That might help the urge to push subside. Help her with her breathing. Tell her to breathe through the urge. Make sure the door's unlocked so I can get right in. I'm in the car now, on my way. Relax, Grandpa, you're doing—"

The line went dead.

★ ★ ★

Thirty-Three Years Earlier

Maria's heartbeat pounded as Jeff lovingly placed the motorcycle helmet on her head. What a beautiful day for a ride. The Colorado sun was shining over the Rockies, and the most handsome man in the universe was taking her for a ride.

She warmed as she remembered their time together last night. She was sore, but the pain was inconsequential. She'd gladly take him to her bed again tonight and every night to come.

"There you go, sweetheart."

Sweetheart. She heated to her toes.

Jeff replaced his own helmet. "Hop on," he said.

She took her seat behind him and grabbed hold of his shirt. His body was hard and warm. She'd never tire of it.

"Where are we going?" she asked.

He twisted his neck and looked into her eyes. "Where *aren't* we going?" He smiled and revved the engine.

Soon they had cruised through town and were out on country roads, free as birds in the sky.

CHAPTER TEN

Shit! Jeff quickly redialed Annie's number. Nothing. Was the door unlocked? Yes, he was sure it was. He couldn't leave Angie.

"Okay, honey," he said. "I'm going to get you ready. Annie's coming, and she'll know what to do. But we're on our own for the next ten minutes."

She gulped and nodded.

Jeff followed Annie's instructions, telling Angie what he was doing as he did it and taking care to cover her with another clean sheet to protect her modesty as he discarded her clothing. When she was lying on her side, he sat by her head, telling her to breathe and relax.

"*You* fucking relax," she said through clenched teeth. "You're not the one trying to push out a watermelon."

Jeff sighed. *Why can't I be more help? Please, Annie, hurry.*

"Daddy, I can't do this breathing anymore. I have to— I have to—" She rolled over onto her back and pulled her legs forward. "I have to push, damn it!" She let out a blood-curdling scream.

"Angie, no! Wait...at least wait for Annie."

She screamed again, her face grimacing in pain. Jeff ran to the foot of the bed. Tentatively, he grabbed the sheet and prepared to lift it.

The doorway opened. "I'm here," Annie called.

Thank God! He let go of the sheet. "We're in here. Hurry!"

Annie rushed into the bedroom. She peeked under the sheet. "Yup. She's crowning. This baby's coming, that's for sure. Hold her hand, Jeff. I just need to wash my hands. I'll only be a second."

Jeff's heart beat like a stampede racing inside him, but his little girl needed him. He placed one hand on her swollen belly. "I'm here, honey. I'm here."

Annie returned, and another scream wrenched from Angie's throat.

"More of the baby's head is coming," she said. "Jeff, I need some clean towels, please."

He tried to let go of Angie's hand.

"No, Daddy. Don't leave me."

Her words melted into him. "I'll be back in a flash. I promise."

He grabbed as many towels as he could hold from the linen closet and returned.

Annie had moved Angie to the end of the bed and was kneeling between her legs. "One more push, Angie, and I think you'll get the head."

"God, I can't." She turned to Jeff. "Daddy. It hurts too much. And I'm so tired."

"I know, honey, but you have to do it. Your baby needs you." He took her clammy hand in his own again. "You're so strong, Angie. You can do anything."

She leaned forward and gritted her teeth, and then came the biggest scream of all.

"That's it, Angie!" Annie's smile spread across her whole face. "The head's out."

Jeff squeezed her hand and looked into his daughter's

green eyes. "You did it, honey! You did it! The head's out. It'll be easy from here."

"Just give me one more," Annie said. "You'll have your baby."

Angie grimaced, her face scarlet, and pushed once more.

"He's here." Annie smiled. "Your little boy is here and he's perfect."

The baby let out a howl.

"And he's breathing!"

"Daddy, I want to see him."

Annie held the baby so she could see. "He's still attached to the cord inside you."

Jeff's head swam. His grandson. He had a grandson.

"We're not quite done," Annie said. "I'll need to deliver the placenta and get him cleaned up, and then you can hold him, okay? Jeff, get me some more towels, damp this time."

He needed every ounce of strength to leave his daughter's side. Jeff ran to the kitchen and wet down some towels. Why hadn't he boiled that damn water? Course it would have been too hot for the newborn baby.

Newborn baby. He hadn't been there for his little girl, but damn it, he'd be there for her son.

When he returned to the bedroom, Annie was holding the squalling little boy. She handed him a pair of scissors from her vet bag. "Care to cut the cord, Grandpa?"

He blinked back tears as he took the scissors and cut the cord, separating his grandchild from his daughter.

Annie washed the baby with one of the damp cloths, wrapped him in a dry towel, and handed him to Angie. "Congratulations, Mom. He's perfect."

Angie took her baby eagerly, tears in her eyes. "Oh, thank

you. Thank you, Annie. And thank you, Daddy. I don't know what I'd have done if you hadn't been here."

Sirens interrupted. Within seconds, two paramedics bombarded the scene. They got Angie and the new baby onto a stretcher and out the door.

"Your husband can go in the ambulance with you, ma'am," one of the techs said.

"He's not here. He's on his way." She looked at Jeff. "Will you come with me, Daddy?"

He smiled, his heart melting. "Of course, sweetheart. Of course."

★ ★ ★

Thirty-Three Years Earlier

"Where are we?" Maria asked, after Jeff stopped the bike. All around her were gorgeous peach trees. Palisade or Fruita, she imagined.

"Palisade. The peach trees after the harvest. I love it here." Jeff took off his helmet and hung it by the strap on his handlebars.

Maria followed suit. She inhaled the sweet fragrance of peaches. She'd never imagined a man like Jeff would be moved by something as simple as a peach orchard, but there he stood, his eyes closed, his deep chest expanding as he inhaled the fragrant aroma.

Maria closed her eyes as well. Nothing better than a ripe western slope peach. Except maybe a ripe western slope Fuji apple. No, the peach was definitely better.

"You like peaches, Jeff?"

He opened his eyes and nodded. "We grow them on Bay

Crossing, but we're mostly beef ranchers. Our fruit can't hold a candle to the stuff here in Palisade. Course my grandpa and brother swear we grow the best ones. Personally, I'd take a Palisade peach over a Bay Crossing peach any day."

"Come on. I bet yours are great."

"Well, they're not mine, first of all. None of it's mine anymore."

Maria winced. She hadn't meant to bring that up. "Then we'll come here to get our peaches." *Oops!* She clasped her hand to her mouth. She'd said too much. How presumptuous could she be? She didn't want to scare Jeff away.

She'd fallen madly in love with Jeff in one day, but she knew better than to think he was feeling the same way.

His strong hands gripped her shoulders and his smoky gaze met hers. "Yes, we'll get our peaches here, Mia."

And then his lips were on hers, sliding, coaxing her open, diving in, and consuming her. She reveled in the kiss, in Jeff, in the orchard, in the vibrant blue sky. Perfection. Simply perfection.

He broke the kiss and nipped at her cheeks and her neck. "Mia," he whispered into her ear. "How can I feel like this?"

She had no answer. After a day? To be in love with him was ridiculous. Yet she was. With all her heart. It was as true as the kiss they'd just shared. The pure truth.

"Mia," he said again, nibbling at her earlobe, "there's something so special about you. So perfect."

I love you, Jeff! How she wanted to cry out the words so they floated up to the azure heavens and then rained down on the entire earth. But she couldn't. It was too soon. She'd scare him away.

Instead, she simply sighed against his warm neck. She

inhaled his musky scent. She'd never tire of his woodsy fragrance.

He found her lips once more and consumed her again.

CHAPTER ELEVEN

Once Angie was settled in her room in the hospital and her little boy had been taken to be weighed and measured, Jeff breathed a sigh of relief. Rafe was less than an hour away now. He would take good care of Angie.

Jeff walked down the hall and through the lobby to the small coffee shop near the hospital entrance. He ordered a black coffee, then stood and sipped it, staring at nothing in particular. A jolt of contentment speared through him. *A grandson.* Jeff Bay had a grandson.

"Hello, Jeff."

Jeff's eyebrows shot up at the familiar voice. He turned to regard a man he hadn't laid eyes on in three decades. He'd put on some weight, and his hair was mostly gray now, but the hazel eyes were the same.

"Max?"

The man didn't smile. "The one and only."

"How are you, man?"

"Been better."

Jeff's heartbeat thumped. He remembered that look in Max's eyes. This wasn't going to lead to anything good.

"So they let you out," Max said.

"Yup. They did. I was innocent, after all."

"Word is that DNA evidence exonerated you."

"Yeah. There was blood on the gun. Turns out it wasn't mine."

"Why would they let out a guy who pleaded guilty?"

"Because I was innocent, that's why. I copped a plea. It happens all the time. It was a stupid decision, but I felt I had no choice at the time. Plus, I got out for good behavior and time served. I was there over thirty years, for God's sake. I did my time. Especially considering I was innocent."

"I think you and I both know whose blood was on that gun."

Yes, Jeff knew. Neither sample had belonged to him. However, one sample was very similar to his—the one that had given him the chance to go to prison after he thought Mia had betrayed him, the one that he'd petitioned the court to have re-examined when DNA tests later became more accurate. The one that, even though he'd confessed at the time, had given him the ability to recant his confession and get released on parole for good behavior.

The other belonged to Max.

"What are we gonna do about this, Jeff?"

"We? You must mean the royal we. I did over thirty years' time for a crime I didn't fucking commit. I'm done doing anything about this."

Max grabbed his collar. "Look, shithead, that was thirty years ago, and I'm not going down for something stupid I did then. I got out twenty-five years ago, and I've made a life for myself. I've got a family now. So you keep your fuckin' mouth shut, got it?"

Jeff broke Max's hold easily. Yeah, he'd learned a lot in prison, and the first lesson had been how to break a hold. He clenched his teeth, his anger turning to red rage. "Don't you dare threaten me. You have a family. I never had the chance for one. I did time for your crime, asshole. You should be down on your knees, thanking me."

"Yeah, I never quite understood why you did that, until I heard that your brother had knocked up your little slut girlfriend. Must have been hard knowing Wayne's dick had been inside your sweet thing."

Rage boiled in Jeff. "You have a funny way of asking for a guy's cooperation, friend."

Max cleared his throat. "I'm not asking. I'm telling. You tell a goddamned soul what really went down that night, and you can kiss your sweet little Angie—and your new grandson—good-bye. As for your Mia? She'll be a goner too, after I have my way with that hot body. Damn, she still looks good after all these years, doesn't she?"

That was all it took. Jeff grabbed Max's collar and was ready to smash his face in with his fist when he remembered he was in a hospital—a hospital where his daughter and grandson were. He unclamped his fists. "You're not worth it."

"I knew you'd see reason. But mark my words. You say anything, and your family will pay the price."

"You'd deny me my family? After all this time? After you just told me you have one of your own?"

"Damn right. I got where I am today by looking out for number one. You're the one who always put someone else first. It got you thirty years. I'm not going to the slammer at age fifty-six, damn it. That was a long time ago. It's not who I am anymore."

Right. What a crock. Jeff wanted to pummel Max's pock-marked face. If anyone ever laid a hand on Angie or Mia...or God forbid, that beautiful baby boy... Then Jeff would actually kill someone for real. He took a deep breath and gathered his strength. It took every bit of restraint he possessed not to put his fist through Max's teeth.

"You just threatened my daughter and her mother. I'd say you're still very much the same person."

"Hey, people revert to old ways when their lives are threatened."

"Look, I didn't rat on you all those years, why would I start now? Is your DNA on record anywhere? Has anyone come looking for you? This is old news, Max. Jesus. Let it go."

"Well, I would, but something in my gut tells me you can't be trusted, Bay."

"Why the fuck would you say that? Did I mention it at all during my incarceration? Fuck you, Max. Fuck you to hell."

"Save your swearing. Just know this. If I get any line that someone's looking for me, or if I get called in, you're gonna pay. Got it?"

"Yeah, right." Jeff shook his head. He lifted his fist, inhaled, and held himself back. "Like I haven't paid enough as it is. Get the fuck out of here, Max. If I see your ugly mug again I *will* turn you in. How's that?"

Max turned and left. Jeff's heart thudded. He didn't trust Max. Not as far as he could throw him. And that didn't sit well with him at all. It stuck in his craw.

Because now he had something to protect.

He had a family.

★ ★ ★

Thirty-Three Years Earlier

"Can I see you tonight? Again?"

Maria inhaled. Kissing Jeff had stolen her breath. He wanted to see her tonight? Heck, he could see her whenever he wanted. As far as she was concerned, she was his. For all time.

But Meghan...

"You mean go out?"

"Well...sure, if you want to." He hedged a little. "But I meant, be together. You know. Like last night."

She gulped. That's what she'd hoped he meant. Of course it would be nice to go out too.

He smiled. "But I'd love to take you out. You want to eat somewhere?"

"Yeah. Sure. I could eat." Though right now her tummy was in knotty flutters.

"Then maybe after...?"

She could hardly catch her breath. But no, not at her house again. Not with Meghan in the next room. Plus, she was a little sore.

"My sister," she said. "I can't do it with her in the next room again. I shouldn't have last night. It was too close a call."

"Of course. I understand." He smiled and cupped her cheek. "I'll take you to my apartment."

His apartment? The thought evoked both excitement and fear. "Mom leaves for work at six, and I should be home with Meghan."

He nodded. "I can't say I'm not disappointed, but I understand."

A jolt of fear struck her. What if he only wanted the sex? "You still want to have dinner?"

He stroked her cheek with his thumb. "Of course. I'm not just after sex with you, Mia. Though that was sure fun."

Yes, it had been fun. But it had been so much more than that. Had it been more for him too?

CHAPTER TWELVE

Maria's soft gaze met his. "Angie and Rafe want to see you."

"Is everything okay?"

"Yes." She smiled. "Everything's fine. The baby's fine. Go on in."

Jeff ambled to the room, wiping all thoughts of Max and his threats from his mind. Right now, he wanted to concentrate on his daughter and new grandson.

He knocked softly and then opened the door to her room. "Hi there."

"Jeff, please come in," Rafe said.

He entered.

"I haven't had the chance to properly thank you for what you did." Rafe grabbed him in a big bear hug.

The act of closeness startled Jeff. His family hadn't been huggers. He'd never embraced his brother or his grandfather. Maybe his father before he'd died. He couldn't remember.

But hugging his son-in-law—the man who took care of his daughter, who loved her, who'd helped her give him his beautiful new grandson—felt good. Felt right. He returned the affection.

"It was nothing. Anyone would have done the same."

Rafe let him go. "I wish I'd been there. I'm just so thankful you were. None of us expected Little Jeff to come so soon."

Jeff gasped without meaning to. Had he heard right? "Little Jeff?"

"Yes, Daddy." Angie smiled. "We've decided to name the baby Jefferson Wayne Bay Grayhawk."

"But what about your father, Rafe?"

"I explained the situation to him, and he was more than understanding. Our next baby will be Jack—or Jacqueline, if it's a girl."

Jeff was flummoxed, awestruck. A lump formed in his throat. "I don't know what to say."

Rafe smiled. "You don't have to say anything. We want to do this. If not for you, Little Jeff might not even be here."

Tears welled in Jeff's eyes. For the love of God, he'd gotten through thirty years of lockdown without shedding a tear, but give him his new family, and he became the damned waterworks.

"I'm honored. Truly. Thank you. Both of you."

Angie smiled. "Would you like to hold your namesake?"

His heart warmed. "Yes. Yes, I'd love to."

As Rafe took the warm bundle from Angie and placed him in Jeff's arms, a new emotion crept into Jeff's heart. *My grandson.* The child was beautiful with a big head of dark hair and dark blue eyes. When those eyes opened and gazed at Jeff, he knew beyond a shadow of a doubt that he would do anything for this child. All the love and devotion he should have been able to lavish on Angie—and that his brother had lavished on her in his absence—he would lavish on Little Jeff. He'd be there for this one. Little Jeff's grandpa might not be able to lavish money on him like Wayne had for Angie, but Little Jeff would not lack for love.

I promise you, he said silently to his grandson. *I promise you everything.*

★ ★ ★

A few days later, back at the ranch, Jeff was currying a horse when the wild berries and vanilla wafted to his nose. He turned.

Mia.

She was a vision. Her onyx hair hung loose around her shoulders, and she wore a simple pair of jeans and a blue-and-white checkered shirt. Her ruby-red lips were curved upward in a slow smile.

"Hello, Jeff."

He couldn't hold back his smile. His grandson, Little Jeff, had melted away the last remaining ice around his heart.

Mia's red lips curved upward. "You're smiling." Her eyes misted, and she sniffed. "That's a real smile. You're just as handsome as you were thirty years ago. Dear God, I thought I'd never see your smile again."

Jeff warmed. Had he truly not smiled at Mia before now? How could he explain it to her or to himself? He couldn't, so he simply said, "He's beautiful, isn't he, Mia?"

Maria wiped at her eyes. "Yes, he sure is. Just as beautiful as Angie was when she was born."

No resentment whirled through him. Not one tiny ounce. He had let his anger at Maria dissipate a while ago, but he'd held on to a shred of it toward his dead brother. Now, he felt only gratitude toward him for taking care of Maria and Angie when he couldn't. He had to be honest with himself. Wayne had given them both more than he could have. Even if he hadn't lied and made a confession, he most likely would have done some time anyway, though not the thirty years he did.

He'd seen photos of Angie as a child, but he'd resisted giving more than a cursory view of all the albums. He was afraid it would hurt too much. Now, he was ready. Maybe he had some more smiles in him. "I'd like to see the pictures, Mia."

Her smile spread across her mouth and lit up her beautiful face. "Really, Jeff?" She threw her arms around him and whispered in his ear, "Thank God. I want you to see all the pictures of her, how beautiful she was, how talented." She backed away, continuing to chatter. "She was the youngest rodeo queen ever crowned in Bakersville, just a few days over eighteen. And so bright. Her IQ is genius level." She tugged at his arm. "Are you done here? Let's go to the house now. Let's look at all the photos together."

He nodded and put away the currycomb. "I'm done. Everything else can wait until tomorrow."

The muscles in his arm jerked, tried to move on their own, to take Maria's smaller hand in his. Yet he held back. Still. No more resentment, but he wasn't a whole man. He feared he would never be. And he wasn't ready to give himself to anyone, not even his Mia.

Especially not his Mia.

"You can stay for supper," she was saying as he followed her out of the barn. "I'm making lasagna. It's already in the oven. And after dinner we'll have a glass of port and pore over all the photos together." She looked over her shoulder and smiled. "You have no idea how much this means to me. Thank you."

★ ★ ★

Thirty-Three Years Earlier

Jeff was happy.

God damn, so that's what the stupid emotion felt like. Across the table, Mia ate her hamburger slowly, her silky neck reddening when some meat juices slid down her chin. She hastily grabbed the napkin from her lap and dabbed at them. Her gaze met his, and then she quickly looked away. How cute. She was embarrassed. He wanted to say something, anything—that he couldn't care less how much food dripped down her chin, but that would embarrass her more.

No, he was satisfied just to look at her and think about how happy he felt just being with her. Never had he felt so good just sitting at the diner with a girl. Never had he actually contemplated—

Damn, can I really go there?

The future? He'd never even considered the future, had never thought past tomorrow. For the first time, he looked forward to the day beyond tomorrow. And he began to feel regret for what he'd allowed himself to become.

Well, a day late and a dollar short. What was done was done. Right now, he'd enjoy watching Mia eat. She was freaking adorable.

A few minutes later, she pushed her plate to the side of the table. "I can't eat another bite. That's one big burger."

"Yeah, they're a good half pound. Haven't you eaten here before?"

"Well..." She reddened again. "We don't really go out to eat very often."

God, he'd stuck his foot in his mouth. Of course she didn't. She lived in a cracker-box house with a mom who worked nights at the convenience store. They were probably lucky to keep food on the table.

"We'll change that, then." He might no longer be an

heir to the Bay fortune, but he did okay. He'd make sure Mia experienced a few of the finer things in life. Though a burger at The Bonnet could hardly qualify as luxury. Next time he'd take her to a real dinner at a real restaurant in the city. What kind of food did she like? No time like the present to find out.

"What's your favorite thing to eat in the world?" he asked.

"That's easy." She smiled. "Mama's beef empanadas. My daddy was Mexican, and he loved my grandma's empanadas. So Grandma taught my mom how to make them, and Daddy said they were even better than Grandma's. But we were sworn to secrecy. Of course, Daddy's gone now."

"I'm sorry. I didn't mean to bring up—"

"Oh, don't be. It's okay. I mean, you lost both your parents. It was doubly worse for you."

Parents. Jeff hadn't thought about them in ages. He'd only been a little kid when they'd died. But they'd been gone a long time. "What happened to your dad? If you don't mind me asking..."

"Car accident. A drunk driver hit him." Her lips quivered. "Ironically, the other driver came out almost unscathed. Just a few scratches."

Drunk driver? What were the odds? Jeff reached across the table and took Maria's hand. "My parents were killed by a drunk driver too."

Her eyes glazed over. "I'm so sorry. How old were you?"

"Pretty little. I hardly remember them." He hated talking about his parents, so he left out any more details. Had they lived, his life might be a lot different today.

"Wow. I was a little older. Ten. But Meghan was only three. She doesn't remember Daddy at all. So you've lived with your grandpa all this time?"

"I moved out when he disinherited me. But otherwise, yeah."

"Can I ask why all that happened?"

"Well, you can ask."

"Oh." She cast a glance down into her lap. "I'm sorry."

"Look," he said, "I like you. I really do. But I hate talking about my family. It's nothing personal. Frankly, I've gotten screwed by my grandpa and my brother. Yeah, I've made a few bad decisions, things golden boy Wayne never would have done. But..." Hell, what else could he say? Maria was a good girl. She wouldn't understand where his head was. He wasn't sure he understood anymore.

Still, he'd promised Max he'd get those combinations...

"It's okay," she said. "We don't have to talk about that. I'm sure you had your reasons for everything you did."

Yeah, well... He'd thought so at the time. Now he wasn't so sure. But damn, Wayne and the old man made him mad as a hungry grizzly! He was just as good as either of them, and he'd show them one way or another.

"So...if they disinherited you—you work, right?"

He smiled. "Yep. I work at the Harley dealership. I sell and fix bikes. It's a decent living. I'm good at it."

"I bet you are." Her eyes lit up and glazed over a bit, as if she were in a trance.

And he melted. In that moment, he knew he'd do anything for this girl. For Mia.

He loved her.

CHAPTER THIRTEEN

"She's beautiful," Jeff said, closing the last photo album. "All three of them are. You and Wayne made beautiful children too."

Maria chewed on her lower lip. Of course, she hadn't been able to show Jeff Angie's photos without showing him photos of Harper and Catie as well. They were all together in albums, along with Wayne himself. She'd considered removing as many of Angie as she could, but decided against it. After all, if Jeff came back to her, he had to know everything. And he had to make peace with everything.

Oddly, he'd seemed to. He and Harper were buddies, as a nephew and uncle should be. And he and Catie adored each other. As for Angie? Maria had noticed she was now calling Jeff "Daddy." All was going fine. He hadn't even winced when he looked at his brother in the photos—not even the photos of Wayne holding a beautiful newborn Angie.

Jeff was healing. Now if only he could forgive her as he had everyone else.

She cleared her throat and stood. "Would you like a glass of wine? I have a wonderful Cab in the cellar. It was one of Wayne's—" She clamped her hand to her mouth.

"One of my brother's favorites, huh?" He grinned. Not one line of displeasure crossed his face. "Well, Wayne always did have the best taste." His gaze swept over her.

She warmed, and the familiar ache between her legs

intensified. How she longed for this man.

"Well?"

"Sure, I'd love a glass. I'm sure I'm not the connoisseur of the finer things in life that Wayne was, but I do enjoy a nice Cab."

Maria winced slightly at his words, but upon studying his face, she again noted no signs of resentment. "Wonderful. I'll get some. I've hardly drunk any wine since Wayne died." She might as well be truthful. "He loved a good tannic red, and he turned me on to them as well."

She rose from the couch and didn't look back for his reaction. When she returned from the cellar with the bottle, he was leafing through the album of Angie as a baby again. The other albums were piled on the coffee table.

"I think Little Jeff looks a lot like her," he said. "Definitely the same nose." He absently glided his fingers along his own nose.

Yes, he and Angie had the same nose. And now Little Jeff would no doubt have it too.

"Yeah, I was thinking the same thing." Maria smiled, uncorked the bottle, and poured two glasses. She handed one to Jeff. "I hope you like it."

He took a sip. "Mmm. Nice flavor. Makes my mouth a little dry."

"That's the tannins."

He nodded, still looking at the photos. "He'll be dark, like Rafe. It's a shame none of your children got your olive complexion, Mia."

She took a sip of wine and let the dry liquid roll over her tongue. "I was surprised too, but they all came out fair like you and Wayne. Remember how fair my mother was?

My daddy was a pretty dark Mexican." She laughed. "Angie always envied me. She wanted to tan in the summer, but all she did was burn, peel, and then she was white again. Catie fared a little better, but Angie and Harp never tanned. She'll be thrilled that Little Jeff has his father's Native American coloring."

Jeff took another sip of wine, his gaze riveted to the photos. He slowly turned page after page of photos he'd already seen, staring at each one as if to memorize it. Which, of course, he probably was. He hadn't seen his daughter as a child. He'd missed so much.

Maria sniffed to hide the tears that wanted to fall. *Get a grip. He needs you to be strong.*

"Are you hungry?" she asked. "I can get something from the kitchen."

He shook his head. "That lasagna hit the spot. You're a good cook, Mia."

She warmed, her cheeks tingling. She was a good cook and she enjoyed doing it, but although Jeff had eaten at her table a few times since he'd come to Bakersville, he'd never once complimented her cooking. Until now.

Dare she hope that things might be getting better between them? The arrival of Little Jeff had no doubt made a big difference. And Jeff had been there for his birth due to circumstance. It seemed only fair, since he hadn't been there for Angie's birth. Maria smiled.

Jeff turned and regarded her.

"Happy, Mia?"

She cleared her throat. "Why would you say that?"

"You had a dreamy smile on your face." He reddened. "The same one I used to see on your face all the time. A long time ago. When you looked at me."

Shivers ran over Maria's skin. She took another sip of wine. Three sips of wine was certainly not enough to make her feel giddy. Nope. It was Jeff. "I was just thinking"—she cleared her throat again—"about how nice it was that you were there for Little Jeff's birth. I mean, if Angie had gone to the hospital, only Rafe would have been allowed in. And it should have been you with me for Angie's birth. It's almost as if...something divine intervened."

Jeff looked away. "I really don't believe in that kind of stuff."

Of course he wouldn't, not after all he'd been through in his life. "I understand. I'm just really glad you could be there for Angie and Little Jeff. And for yourself."

Jeff reached toward her and laid his hand on her forearm. A blaze went through her, as if his touch were fire itself. All these years and nothing had changed. She still responded to his slightest touch.

She gathered her courage and laid her other hand over his. They sat for a moment, touching but not looking at each other, until they both looked up at the same time. Jeff's dark eyes smoldered.

"Mia," he said, his voice husky.

She swallowed. "Jeff?"

"Take me upstairs."

★ ★ ★

Thirty-Three Years Earlier

Crazy as shit, to love someone after a couple of days, but he knew it as sure as he knew his damned grandfather had disinherited him.

He loved Maria Gomez. He loved her onyx hair that fell over her shoulders in silky waves. He loved how she got embarrassed when hamburger juice dripped down her chin. He loved how she felt behind him on his motorcycle, how she adorably and shyly placed her hands on his hips and held on to him. He loved how she cared for her sister and chased away the things that went bump in the night. She'd be a wonderful mother. And most of all, he loved how her lips felt against his when he kissed her, how their bodies molded together as though they'd been created for each other.

But she was young, a good three years younger than he, and only eighteen. He'd have to tread carefully not to scare her.

Good thing she didn't know what he was up to tonight. Because he couldn't be with her, he'd made arrangements to take care of some business—business she definitely wouldn't approve of.

He'd take care of it, but this would be the last time. He was going straight.

For the woman he loved.

★ ★ ★

Jeff stood over his sleeping brother. Regret washed over him, until he remembered Grandpa's will. He shook Wayne awake.

"What? What is it?" Wayne's eyes opened.

"It's me, you horse's ass."

His brother yawned and then sat up in bed. "What the fuck do you want?"

"Just a little information."

"Get the fuck out of here, Jeff. I need my sleep. Some of us get up early around here to do ranch work."

"Cry me a goddamned river."

"I knew I should have had the locks to the house changed. Jesus."

"Well, you didn't. And funny thing is, you're not going to even recall this chat come tomorrow." He held a cup to his brother's mouth. "Drink this."

"Huh?"

"I said drink it."

"Right. And what if I don't?"

Jeff pulled the pistol out of the back of his waistband and pointed it at his brother's forehead. "Then I fucking kill you."

Wayne jerked beneath the gun. "Christ, Jeff, what the fuck are you doing?"

Jeff's hand shook. Was he really holding a gun on his brother? He'd never shoot him. Hell, it wasn't even loaded. But Wayne didn't know that.

"Just drink it, asshole, or I blow your brains out."

"I don't believe you."

Jeff cocked the trigger. Would Wayne call his bluff? "You better start believing."

"If this is poison, you might as well kill me now."

"It's not poison. Trust me, you'll live through this, and you'll go on with your golden boy life. I promise. Now drink it."

"Jeff—"

"I swear to God I'll do it, Wayne." His words sounded a hell of a lot more sure than he actually was. He could never harm his brother. He hated the man, but Jeff was no killer.

But Wayne didn't have to know that at this particular

instant.

Wayne took the cup, his hands shaking visibly. He drank it slowly. "It's bitter."

"Sorry. They were out of the strawberry flavor."

"What is this, anyway?" He gulped the last of it.

"It's ketamine. It'll give you amnesia for about thirty minutes. It will be retroactive for about an hour before now. Then you'll fall back into your dreamy sleep and you'll never know I was here."

Jeff waited about fifteen minutes until Wayne entered a dreamlike state, his eyes glossed over.

"Tell me, Wayne. What are the combinations to Grandpa's safes?"

"The ones in his office or the one in his bedroom?"

He had one in his bedroom? News to Jeff. "All of them."

"Big safe in office, fifty-five, sixty-seven, eight-oh-nine. Smaller one, seventy-eight, oh-six, eighty-nine."

Jeff scribbled the numbers on a piece of paper. "And the one in the bedroom?"

"He never told me."

"Give me a break. He tells you everything."

"He never told me." Wayne slurred his words.

Jeff was certain Wayne would tell him if he knew. He'd divulged the others quick enough. But maybe...

"Come on..."

"He made me promise not to tell."

"Yeah? Well, you're about to break that promise, aren't you?"

"Yeah," Wayne mumbled. "It's twenty-one, forty-three, twenty-one. But I don't know what's in there. He made me promise never to look in there."

"Well, it's a good thing I never made such a promise," Jeff said. "Thanks, bro. You've been very helpful. Now just go on to sleep, and you'll wake up fit as a fiddle with no recollection of this little talk."

"'Kay, Jeff. Night." Wayne closed his eyes and let out a snore.

Jeff clutched the paper with the combinations written on it in his sweaty palm.

And a light bulb turned on in his head. Why the fuck was he thinking about sharing this shit with that low-life Max? This was *his* inheritance, not theirs. And here he was in the house with Grandpa still in the hospital and Wayne out cold. Surely it wouldn't hurt to have a look.

He walked toward his grandfather's bedroom. Where would the safe be? Probably behind one of the fake Impressionist paintings Norman was so fond of. He checked the one above the bed first. No dice. Then the one over his dresser. Nothing. Lastly, the one on the wall facing the bed. Pay dirt—a safe, built right into the wall.

He removed the painting from the wall and reached to touch the safe, when he realized his fingerprints would be everywhere. Fuck. He'd ruined this already. No way could he open this safe now. He'd have to come back with gloves.

But his curiosity nagged at him. Even Wayne didn't know what was in this safe. Damn. What could Norman be hiding in here?

But no. Not worth it. He couldn't risk his prints being anywhere on the safe. They were already on the frame of the painting. He walked to Grandpa's dresser and fumbled around, finding a pair of socks. Quickly he brushed them over the frame of the painting, rubbing hard, hoping he was at least marring the oil of his prints enough so they wouldn't be recognizable should it occur to anyone to look there.

What the fuck? He'd share the info with Max and the gang. Yeah, they were low-life scum, but they'd been his brothers when his own brother had written him off. Plus, it wouldn't hurt to have back up.

He left the room and walked back by Wayne's bedroom. Still out cold.

A boulder of guilt gripped him and he entered the room again. He put his hand to Wayne's neck. Thank God. His pulse was strong. He'd be okay.

Jesus Christ! I just drugged my brother! What kind of an animal was he?

He'd promised the boys he'd help them rob Norman. Old Norman deserved what he got. But that would be his last crime. After that, he was going straight. He wanted a life he could be proud of, a life Mia could be proud of.

He was going to propose to her.

He imagined a little girl with his light skin and Mia's ebony hair. What a beauty. She'd have brown eyes, no doubt. Both he and Mia had brown eyes. Big brown doe eyes, his little girl.

He smiled and left Wayne's bedroom, stalked down the hall quietly, through the living room and out the back door where he left it locked as if no one had been there.

He didn't go home.

CHAPTER FOURTEEN

Jeff gazed into Mia's eyes as he unbuttoned her shirt and eased it off her shoulders. It fell in a checkered pool at her feet. His touch was like fire, igniting her skin as he grazed his fingers up her arms to her bra straps, and then eased them over her shoulders too. With one hand, he reached behind her and unclasped the garment. It joined the blouse on the floor. Her ample breasts fell gently against her chest. Her brown nipples were already rigid, eager for his attention.

"Still so beautiful, Mia," he said. "You haven't changed at all."

She heated and knew ruddiness was spreading over her cheeks and bosom. She looked down. "I've given birth to three children and aged thirty-plus years. I've changed." Not to mention the twenty or more pounds she was carrying since they'd last made love.

He cupped her cheek and drew her gaze to his. "You haven't changed to me."

She nearly melted to a pool of syrup on the floor among her discarded clothes.

Jeff glided a finger along her jawline, down the contours of her neck, to her shoulder. Maria quivered. He avoided her breasts, though she ached for him to touch them. His finger followed her upper arm to her lower arm, until he reached her hand and clasped it.

Gathering her courage, she brought his hand to her

breast. "Touch me, Jeff."

He cupped one heavy globe and squeezed it gently. "God, Mia."

"Oh, Jeff"—she leaned into him—"I've missed you so much."

"Mia." He leaned down and crushed his mouth to hers.

They'd kissed once before, in the kitchen, but this kiss held so much more. This kiss held promise, and Mia gave herself to the moment—gave herself to Jeff. She'd always belonged to Jeff, always, even all those years she'd spent with his brother. She'd never been Wayne's. Only Jeff's.

Their lips slid together and their tongues tangled. Jeff tasted of the tannic red wine they'd shared, and she drank of him, let his essence pour into her and fill the emptiness that had tormented her for so long.

But Jeff...was he sure? He'd resisted her for so long, even when she'd brazenly come to him in the middle of the night. Maria had to make sure this was what he wanted. Though it pained her, she forced her mouth away from his.

"Mia?" he said tentatively.

She wiped her mouth, her legs unsteady. "Are you sure, Jeff? I just don't want to push you. I know things have been—"

"Yeah, yeah." He had a hard time breathing. "I'm sure. I want this." Jeff gripped her shoulders so hard she was afraid he might leave a mark. "I'm so sure, Mia. I can't stay away from you one minute longer. I'm not sure why I waited this long."

He pulled her close, and his hardness pushed into her tummy. How she'd missed him. She wanted to touch him everywhere, lick him everywhere. She wanted to rip his clothes off, and then her own, and make love right there on the floor.

"You're so beautiful, Mia." He cupped her face in his hands. "Your black eyelashes are as long as I remember." He pushed his erection into her. "Do you feel that?"

"Yes."

"Feel how much I hunger for you. I want you so much."

Her breathing was unsteady, coming in rapid pants. Her heart slammed against her sternum.

"Do you want me?"

"God, Jeff. Yes."

"Will you say it for me, Mia? Say you want me."

She poured her whole heart and soul into her next three words, hoping he could see the truth in her gaze. "I want you."

His mouth, reckless and possessive, claimed hers. He swept her into his arms and carried her to the bed. He caressed her shoulders, her breasts, lightly pinching each nipple. She gasped as her blood boiled. With each touch, he ignited more heat within her, all the way down to her core between her legs. She was wet. She could tell. So wet for him. It had been so, so long.

He moved slowly as he unbuttoned her jeans and eased them over her hips, letting his fingers linger over each inch of flesh as he exposed it. She wanted to be naked—naked under his touch. She wriggled and groaned, whispering his name.

"Please," she said, and found herself repeating the word again and again.

"Please what, my Mia?" he rasped.

"I...don't know."

"Do you want me to touch you?"

"Yes, please."

"Here?"

He ran his fingers lightly over her belly. She squirmed. He trailed lower, through her dark curls to her clit. She jolted.

"Here?"

"Oh yes," she said, sighing.

He slid through her folds. "You're wet for me, Mia. God, always so wet for me."

She quivered, her mind whirling and wheeling. For a moment, she was back in her bedroom in her mother's old house, being touched by Jeff for the first time. She opened her eyes and then closed them. Opened them again. Thoughts were impossible. Only feelings coursed through her.

"Wet. For you. Yes, Jeff, only for you." And once more, as always with Jeff, the truth hit her. "Only you, Jeff. I never got wet for anyone else."

His fingers stopped their work. She mourned their absence, but when his gaze met hers, his eyes misted over with tears, her heart melted.

"Is that true, Mia?"

Truth. She'd only had pure truth with Jeff and no other. And she was truthful now. "Yes, Jeff. I promise. I only got wet for you. With Wayne, the first time, it was painful."

He winced. "I'm sorry."

"We used lubricant. And we weren't very...sexually active. Ever, really. And not at all after Catie came along."

A crooked smile emerged on his full pink lips. "I can't say I'm sorry to hear that."

Maria grabbed his cheeks and pulled his handsome face toward hers. "Believe me when I tell you, Jeff. It was always you. There was never anyone else for me. Ever."

"Oh, Mia." His mouth clamped down on hers.

The kiss was possessive again, but not as reckless this

time. It was deliberate and sensual...and true. Their tongues tangled together as they made love with their mouths. Jeff's erection poked at Maria's thigh. She wished he had taken his clothes off.

When she turned away to take a much-needed breath, she said, "You have too many clothes on."

He chuckled. "I couldn't agree more." He stood and unbuttoned his shirt, and with each button came golden skin and dark chest hair. He was so gorgeous, the epitome of what a man should be. He was always so handsome, so masculine. Time hadn't affected his manliness at all.

Her skin erupted in tiny bumps as she gulped with each further inch of exposed flesh. When he unzipped his jeans, she caught her breath. He toed off his boots and slid the jeans and boxers over his hips.

She gasped when his cock sprang free. It was as beautiful as she remembered—still with one purple vein decorating the shaft. Strange that she remembered each curve of that vein, like a meandering river. But she did. She remembered every centimeter of him.

He finished removing her jeans and lay next to her on the bed. His warmth flooded her, cocooned her, made her feel safe.

Made her feel loved.

Love.

He hadn't said the words. She longed to hear them, but she wouldn't push. She was thrilled that he'd come back to her bed, and she didn't intend to waste a minute of it.

He kissed her again, while his strong, callused fingers toyed with her delicate folds. She moved against him, finding his rhythm, arching her hips in need.

Jeff flipped her onto her back and slid down her body, tracing her skin with his tongue as he went. Every nerve inside her sizzled. He kissed her neck, her chest, the plump swells of her breasts, her nipples, her belly. He swirled his tongue in her navel, and then lower...

She arched and cried out as he flicked his tongue over the sensitive bud of her clit.

"So long," he said against her rigid flesh. "So long I've dreamed of tasting you again." He slid his tongue over her dewy folds. "You're so pretty down here. So plump and pink. I could look at you forever." He grinned up at her, his chin glistening with her juices. "But I'd rather eat you."

His coarse words evoked a memory and awakened every cell in her body. "Oh, Jeff. Please. Please."

He dived into her sex, pulling at her labia, tonguing her clit and her opening. Maria grasped the bed sheets, arched her back, moved her hips to help him find the perfect spot to—

She shattered. A kaleidoscope of emotion too long dead whirled into her, beginning between her legs and radiating through her body all the way to her fingertips and toes. She heated, cooled, heated again. He continued his passionate assault. She climaxed again, and then again. Just when she thought she couldn't take one more second of this exquisite torture, he pushed two fingers inside her slick channel, and she flew again into the throes of ecstasy.

When she landed back into reality, he was fingering her, slowly, deliberately, bringing her down. "You're beautiful when you come, Mia."

"Oh, Jeff." Tears filled her eyes. "Jeff. I can't believe it."

He kissed her swollen sex and climbed up to her. "Don't cry."

She shook her head. "It's a good cry. I promise. It's just..."

He kissed her lips softly, his lips laced with her own tangy sweetness. "What?"

"Thirty-three years, Jeff. Thirty-three years since I've felt that."

He grinned. "We always were dynamite together."

She shook her head again. "No. I mean, yes. We were. We are." Her words came out jumbled as she tried to get her mind to stop swirling from the nirvana she'd just experienced. "But that's not what I meant." She closed her eyes, inhaled. Opened them again and met his chocolate gaze. He had to know. He had to know the truth of what he meant to her. Had always meant to her.

"I mean, I haven't had an orgasm in thirty-three years."

★ ★ ★

Thirty-Three Years Earlier

Jeff rapped softly on Maria's window. She was no doubt asleep. He didn't want to scare her, but he had to see her. Had to feel her in his arms. Had to know she was there, that something was worth fighting for. He'd pull this one last job. Grandpa deserved it anyway. After that, he'd take Mia, and they'd build a life together. A good, honest life.

The window opened. "Jeff?" Mia peeked out, her hair in adorable disarray.

"God, you're beautiful. You take my breath away, Mia." Already he was hardening inside his jeans.

"I told you I couldn't—"

He silenced her, placing two fingers against her trembling lips. "I know. I'm sorry. I just had to see you. I had to look into your beautiful eyes."

She reached up and joined her hand to his. "Are you okay?"

He smiled. Yes, he was okay, now that he was with her. In her presence. He was no longer Jeff Bay, disinherited criminal. He was Jeff Bay, a good man, a man who would do anything for the woman he loved.

Soon, she would be his. He'd admit his love and take her away from all this. They'd build a life together. Have children together...

"Jeff?" she said again.

"I'm fine. Really. Can I come in? Just for a minute?"

She sighed and opened the window fully. "I can't seem to say no to you."

He climbed in. Maria sat down on her bed, and he sat beside her.

"I've missed you."

"You just saw me tonight." She laughed softly.

"What time is it, anyway?"

Maria glanced at her nightstand. "A little after two."

"Your sister's safe in bed?"

She nodded. "Tucked her in myself four hours ago."

"I'm sorry I woke you."

"Actually, I wasn't asleep. Just lying here...thinking."

He smiled and touched the soft apple of her cheek. "About what?"

She looked away. "About...you. About us."

His hand still on her cheek, he turned her toward him. "What about us?"

Even in the darkness of her bedroom, her face blushed a delicate rose. "I don't know. I had a nice time tonight. I have so much fun with you. It feels..."

"Feels like what?" he urged.

She stayed silent.

His heart was beating so fast, like a herd of buffalo was stampeding inside him. "Can I tell you how I feel, Mia?"

Her lips quivered as she nodded.

He claimed her other cheek with his remaining hand. He looked straight into her warm brown eyes.

Could he say it? He cleared his throat, his nerves jumping. *Get a grip, Bay.*

She widened her eyes slightly, expectantly. She said nothing.

He gathered every ounce of courage he possessed and spoke from pure emotion. "Mia, I love you."

CHAPTER FIFTEEN

Jeff's eyes widened to saucers. "What?"

She swallowed. She wasn't frigid. She just hadn't let herself. Hadn't wanted... A memory long buried jerked into her mind. Her last time with Jeff, in her bedroom, all those years ago... Her last orgasm, and the fleeting thought that she'd never feel that way again...

Thirty-three years...

"Was my brother that bad in bed? God." Jeff exhaled, slowly shaking his head.

"No. I mean, he was fine. He just wasn't *you*."

"He couldn't make you come?"

"You're not understanding me." She cupped his face. "I didn't let myself. I didn't want to climax. Not with anyone but you."

His lips parted, and astonishment crept over his face. "Mia?"

"It was my choice."

"But I—"

She silenced him, touching two fingers to his soft lips. "It's okay. I don't expect that you did the same. I know men have...needs."

His neck reddened. "Oh, God."

"Jeff, I told you, it's okay. Everything is okay. It doesn't matter. Women. Men. I know how things are in prisons..."

Jeff sat up and swung his legs over the side of the bed.

"Mia, I hope to God for your sake that you *don't* know how things are in prison. I didn't have any relationships. No women and certainly not any men. I managed to escape...*that.* The only sexual release I got was whacking off, and trust me, that was pretty rare."

Maria touched his upper arm. He had turned cold as ice. *Lord, what have I done?* She stayed silent as her heart fell to her tummy.

"Prison is not conducive to... Oh, fuck." He stood and grabbed his boxers and jeans from the floor. "I can't do this right now."

"Jeff, please."

He turned to her, his face ashen. "I saw things there. Heard things. Really didn't put me in any kind of sexual mood. Not even good old teenaged yanking." He stepped into his boxers and then his jeans. "I have to go."

She stood, went to him, and grasped him against her. "Jeff, don't go."

He shook her off. "I have to."

She threw herself against him again, determined. "No, you don't. I'm here. I'm here for you. I want you just as you are. I don't care about any of that."

He untangled himself from her, turned her to face him, and looked her straight in the eyes, his gaze burning. "You're not hearing me. I can't. Not now. Not with— Damn!" He shook his head. "Too many demons to face."

"Demons? Jeff, what are you—"

"I'm done talking tonight." He zipped his jeans, grabbed his boots and shirt, and stomped out of the bedroom.

Mia fought the urge to follow, to beg. She wanted him, but not like this. Jeff, for whatever reason, needed to be alone.

She fell back into bed and cried herself to sleep.

★ ★ ★

Thirty-Three Years Earlier

Maria froze, gulped. He loved her? Her insides turned to mush. *He loves me!*

Jeff fidgeted next to her. "I just poured my heart out here. Aren't you going to say anything?"

Wasn't she smiling? She touched her lips. She must have been too shocked to smile. Elation overwhelmed her. She curved her lips upward in what she hoped was her biggest smile ever. Love for Jeff threatened to spill out of her. "Jeff, I love you too."

He exhaled audibly. "Thank God."

She laughed, softly, so as not to wake Meghan in the next room. "Did you think I didn't?"

"I don't know. I mean, we only just met and all, but it feels—"

"Right," she finished for him. "It feels right, Jeff."

He grinned, his hands on her face again. "Yeah. Yeah, it sure does." He leaned forward and brushed his lips against hers. "I'll go now. I don't want to wake your sister." He stood. "Can I see you tomorrow?"

Maria stood and took both his hands in hers. "Of course you can see me tomorrow."

"Okay. Thanks for letting me in tonight." He kissed her again. "I'll see you tomorrow."

No. She didn't want him to leave. They'd be quiet, really quiet. She'd lock the door to her room. Meghan was sleeping soundly. If she woke? Well, Maria would leave the window open so Jeff could get away quickly.

She tugged on his arms. "Stay, Jeff. Please." She pulled him back down on to the bed. "Stay and make love to me."

"Mia." His voice was husky, deep. "God."

He crushed his lips to hers in a frenzy of lips, teeth, and tongue. They kissed quietly but with passion. Maria's whole body blazed with a sensual fever. Her nipples tightened against her tank top and threatened to poke into Jeff's chest. They were so hard, and she longed for him to rip off her tank and suck on them.

He explored her shoulders, her arms, her waist, and finally slid his hands under the soft cotton of her tank and up to her breasts.

"Ah!" She kept her voice low, but his fingers on her nipple felt so good. So right.

"Can you take this off, baby?" Jeff said, but didn't wait for her reply. He glided the material over her torso and head and set it down on the floor next to the bed.

Now naked from the waist up, Maria gazed down at her chest. Her breasts were swollen and rosy, and her nipples stood out like two pencil erasers.

"You're beautiful, Mia, just beautiful." He bent and took a nipple into his mouth.

Maria died a little just then. How else could she explain the heaven she felt? He clamped his lips onto her, first teasing, and then sucking, and then he bit her ever so lightly. And she found she wanted more.

"Harder. Bite me harder."

Had she just uttered those words? When he complied, a bolt of lightning hit her clit. Was it possible to climax like this? Probably not, but it was heavenly all the same.

Jeff continued nibbling on her nipple while he tormented the other one with his fingers. He flicked it, twisted it lightly, and then, just as he bit down on the other, he pinched it.

And again the lightning bolt. Although she was sitting, her hips longed to move. She wanted to arch, to thrust, to find his hard cock and impale herself on it—all from just a little breast play.

But Jeff wasn't done with her chest. He cupped both breasts and toyed with the nipples while he glided his lips over the swells of her flesh. He murmured against her how beautiful she was, how hot she made him. How much he wanted her.

"I want you too," she said, her voice breathy. "I want you so much."

He finally lifted his head, still twisting her nipples with his fingers. She squirmed. Staying still was impossible. Her hips needed to move. That empty place inside her needed filling. By him.

He moved one hand from her nipple and slid it down her side to her panties. He eased them off. She helped him, squirming out of them and kicking them to the other side of the room. He touched her between the legs and she nearly exploded.

"You're wet, Mia."

God, yes. She was sure she must be dripping, she was so turned on.

He slid one finger inside her. So sweet. So good. He added another and moved them around, finding a spot that made her want to cry out. But she held it in. She couldn't risk waking Meghan. And she didn't want any of this to stop.

He continued working her with his fingers, his other

hand still pinching her nipple. How much more torture could she take? He kissed her lips, her cheek, her neck, and then whispered in her ear, "Lie back. I want to eat you."

Eat. She'd heard that term. Hadn't actually heard anyone say it though. It was crass. It was sexy. It made her feel...sexy.

She lay back and whimpered a little when his fingers left her nipple. But oh, she'd like what was coming. She knew it instinctively. His lips clamped onto her clit while his fingers still slid slowly in and out of her. He sucked on her tight bud, and she grasped the sheets in her fists and bit down on her lip to keep from screaming his name.

But she couldn't keep totally quiet. She said softly, "Jeff, Jeff. It feels so good."

His groan vibrated against her wet folds. He turned his head and sucked on the delicate skin of her inner thigh. That alone nearly sent her through the roof. And when he returned his mouth to her clit, it happened.

Sky rockets. She thrashed, she gasped, she clung to the sheets with her fists.

From somewhere, Jeff said, "Shh..."

When she came down from her high, he was still fingering her—slowly, slowly—until he slid both fingers out of her.

He came forward and kissed her, deep. "Taste yourself, Mia. Taste yourself on me."

What a heady sensation. She kissed him back, taking all of him in. When she finally broke the kiss to take a breath, she realized he was still fully clothed.

She should be embarrassed. But she wasn't. Not at all. One thing was for sure, though. He needed to get naked.

She tugged at his shirt. He got the message and rose. He shed his shirt, boots, and jeans. Only his boxers remained, his cock tenting them. Slowly he slid them over his hips, and they puddled to the floor. He grabbed a condom out of his jeans pocket and quickly sheathed himself.

"Please, Jeff." She wanted him inside her so badly. "Now."

He wasn't slow this time. Didn't take his time. He lay down on top of her and thrust into her.

Though she had been sore earlier, she felt no pain. Just some exquisite stretching that made her feel complete. She nuzzled into his neck to muffle her sounds. His masculine musky smell only added to her euphoria. *In. Out. In. Out.* Had anything ever felt so good?

"Mia," he whispered against her, "I'm sorry. I can't last much longer."

He plunged into her deeply and grunted. When his pelvic bone hit her clit, she went over the precipice again. She sobbed into his neck, her words muffled, as the release took her.

Heaven, such heaven. For one fearful moment, she wondered if she'd ever feel like this again—this pure joy at joining with another human being. She erased the thought from her mind and flew.

She never wanted to let him go.

CHAPTER SIXTEEN

Jeff sighed, lying in bed. He'd made a huge mess of things with Mia last night. His body weighed him down like an anvil. He didn't want to move.

Until he heard his doorbell.

Probably Harper, wondering where the hell he was this morning. His nephew sure was an early riser. Jeff admired the man. He had a true work ethic. Normally Jeff was right along with him, but this morning he couldn't move.

He'd make it up to Harper. But today he couldn't work. He reached to the nightstand for his cell to give Harper a call and let him know he wouldn't be working today.

Before he could punch in the numbers, his bedroom door opened. Mia stood there, a tray in her hands.

"Good morning," she said. "I thought I'd bring you breakfast today."

He was caught between elation to see her and anger that she'd barged in. Yeah, she was the owner and she had a key, but Christ. Wasn't he entitled to a little privacy?

"Mia—"

"I know. I know. I shouldn't have walked right in. But when you didn't come to the door, I got worried."

"You should have assumed I was working. I should have been up hours ago."

"Harp told me you didn't show up today. I told him you weren't feeling well. I hope I didn't overstep my bounds."

"Overstep your bounds? Christ, yes, Mia, you overstepped your bounds. You've been overstepping your bounds since I got here. I was just about to call Harper. I would have looked like a damn fool."

Her face fell. "I'm sorry."

He shook his head. He could bear anything but that, her sadness. "No, no. It's okay." He swung his feet over the side of his bed. He was dressed only in boxers, but why stand on ceremony? They'd bared all to each other last night. And as much as he wished it weren't, her face was a welcome sight. "I'd be happy to have breakfast with you."

Her smile lit her beautiful features. "Wonderful. I'll set it up at the kitchen table."

"Okay. I'll only be a minute." He went to the bathroom and took care of business, brushed his teeth, and ran his fingers though his unruly hair. *Well, what you see is what you get.* He pulled a pair of jeans over his boxers. Didn't bother with a shirt. The autumn air was fresh and warm.

He studied his reflection in the bathroom mirror. A few lines creased his forehead and the outer edges of his eyes, and silver highlighted his dark hair. His shoulders were still broad and his arms still muscular, and thanks to the hard work on the farm—and admittedly, in the big house—he still had hard pecs and abs. Not bad for his age. Not bad at all.

But damn, he felt like a shithead. He'd walked out on Mia last night, and he hadn't given her any clue why. How could he? She'd never understand. Hell, he didn't understand half of it himself.

No. That was a goddamned lie. He understood all too well. He'd never be whole again.

He sighed and walked out to the kitchen. Mia was dressed

in denim capri pants and a pink blouse that highlighted her olive skin. She looked beautiful, of course. What had he expected?

She was setting out fresh biscuits and honey. "I'm warming the frittata in the microwave. It'll be done—"

The bell on the microwave dinged.

"—now." She pulled a plate of eggs out.

Jeff inhaled. Mmm. Smelled like ham and mushroom. His stomach growled. He was surprised he felt hungry. "Smells good."

"Thanks. I hope you like it." She opened the refrigerator. "Do you have any salsa?"

"Yeah, look inside the door."

Maria grabbed it and set it on the table. "I'll bring you some of my homemade salsa later. But this will do for now." She opened a carafe of coffee she'd brought and poured two cups. "Come on. Sit down."

Jeff obeyed.

Maria sat across from him. Distance—she was maintaining distance. It was as apparent as the sun in the sky.

She cleared her throat. "I want to apologize—"

"For barging into my house?"

"No." She reddened. "I mean, yes, of course."

God she was beautiful.

"But also for last night. I didn't mean to..."

Strangely, he understood her hesitation. "Hard to find the words, isn't it?"

She nodded.

"Look, Maria. There are some things you're never going to understand. Things I can't even explain. Things I don't know if..." He sighed. Words escaped him.

"Jeff, if you need to talk—"

He pounded his fist on the table. She jumped.

"Hell, yes, I need to talk. And I need to be silent. And I need so many fucking things..." He buried his head in his hands.

Maria rose. The patter of her footsteps came near, and then her lips touched the top of his head.

"I wish I could help, Jeff. I wish I could chase away those demons for you. I may not be able to, but I could at least try. If you let me in."

★ ★ ★

Thirty-Three Years Earlier

"Are you sure your brother's not home?"

"Yeah. He went out. On a date I think," Jeff scoffed. "Some high society deb from Denver who's in town visiting relatives."

"Could be you'll have a new sister-in-law soon." Max laughed.

"Where are the others?"

"Booker's home sick. Trey should be here soon." Max checked his watch. "Jesus, where the fuck is he?"

Jeff scanned the premises. "There he is."

Trey Dodson loped up, dressed all in black, as they all were. "Hey, sorry I'm late."

"Shouldn't be a problem," Jeff said. "Gramps is still in the hospital, and Wayne's out. Let's move and get this over with."

Jeff keyed open the door, and they went inside Casa Bay.

"No alarm?" Trey asked.

Jeff shook his head. "Nope. Though I'm sure one will be installed first thing tomorrow."

"Where's the loot?" Max said.

"In the old man's den. Come on."

Jeff led them to Grandpa Norman's office. The room was spacious. Paintings of livestock peppered the walls, and the furniture was fine mahogany. Papers covered his sprawling desk. Jeff glanced quickly over them, and one caught his eye. *Codicil.* That was an addition to a will, right? Was Gramps changing his will? Maybe writing him back in? He picked up the paper and scanned through it, squinting his eyes in the darkness. A lot of legal jargon about daughters being married or something.

So he was still disinherited. Fuck the old bastard. Jeff was all in now. He'd get his rightful due one way or another.

"What are you reading that shit for?" Max said. "Let's get moving. Loverboy might get back early."

Max was right. Jeff tossed the document in the trash. Gramps no doubt had copies. Or his lawyer did. Who gave a rat's ass anyway?

He moved behind the desk and removed the bust of the head of Michelangelo's *David*—Grandpa's taste in art was eclectic, the Renaissance and cattle—and some stray books from the top of the big safe. The big bucks wouldn't be here. They'd be in the wall safe hidden behind the copy of Leonardo da Vinci's *The Last Supper*. But Jeff had made up his mind to start in this safe. He'd always wondered what Gramps hid inside.

Carefully he turned the combination lock back and forth, hitting each number. He pulled the door open slowly.

"Shine the light over here, Trey," he said.

The beam illuminated first several piles of stock certificates. No good. They needed liquid. He pulled out the stocks and pushed them aside. Next he pulled out a cedar box the size of a loaf of bread. He opened it.

Jewels! Had they belonged to his grandmother? Or, God forbid, his mother?

He pushed the thought from his mind. Mom and Grandma were gone, and he was here to get his due.

A string of small pearls caught his eye. In his mind, Mia was wearing them, their white sheen a beautiful contrast to her tan skin. He grabbed them and pocketed them, and then said, "Check these out, guys. They'll be worth a buck or two." He handed the box to Max and continued searching.

He pulled out a pocket watch. An old pipe. The old man smoked a pipe? Or maybe this had belonged to someone important. He tossed it aside. In the back were stacks of bills. Show time! They were hundreds. About twenty packs of hundreds, each totaling ten thousand dollars.

He'd hit the fucking jackpot.

He shoved one in his pocket with the necklace and tossed the others out to the guys. "Pay dirt, fellas."

"Shit the bed," Max said. "There's two or three hundred grand here. And you said the big money ain't in this safe?"

"I said it's probably not in this safe. My guess is it's in the wall safe." He deliberately didn't mention the safe in Grandpa's bedroom. That was for his eyes and his eyes alone. He just had to figure out when to check it out.

Only a couple of gold coins were left in the safe. He pocketed one—hell, he was related to the man and these others were nothing to Grandpa Norman—and threw the rest to the guys.

"That cleans this out."

"Where's the other safe?"

Jeff stood. "It's over there." He pointed to the Leonardo painting. "Behind *The Last Supper*."

Trey beamed the light on the painting. "What are we waiting for?"

"Yeah, Bay," Max said. "Let's quit fucking around."

"Who's fucking around?" Jeff put the stock certificates and pipe back into the safe and replaced the books and statue. He walked to the painting and ran his gloved hand over the top of the frame. His fingertip was coated in dust. Whoever Gramps was paying to clean his house sucked. For some reason, the thought made him laugh out loud.

"What's so funny?" Max said.

Jeff shook his head. "Nothing." He prepared to lift the painting and then jerked when a voice invaded his thoughts.

"What the fuck do you think you're doing?"

CHAPTER SEVENTEEN

Let her in? Jeff shook his head. "You don't want to be let in to this hell, Mia. Trust me."

Still behind him, she wrapped her arms around his neck and kissed his head again. "I won't pretend to understand what you've been through. I know I can't. But I want to help. Sometimes you just need to let it out."

"Oh, God." His face hit his hands again. *Damn it!* He was not going to cry. *Not going to be weak. Weakness gets you killed.*

"It's okay, Jeff." Her lips touched his head once more. "Let it out. It's okay."

But it wasn't okay. It would never be okay. His shoulders shook as the unwanted tear fell into his hands.

Mia's comforting hands caressed his shoulders. Then she curved her arms around him, tighter this time. Her lips slid over his neck. She said nothing.

A giant sob racked through him. He heard his own voice crying—like an echo, as if the sounds were coming from far away. He hated it, but he was powerless to stop the onslaught. It was coming out now, and he no longer had any control.

Mia loosened her hold and knelt down next to him, combing her fingers through his hair. He looked up, knowing his face was red and tear-stained.

She had tears in her eyes too. *No!* That's the last thing he wanted, for her to hurt. He pushed the chair back, its legs squeaking against the tile floor, and stood. "Mia, you have to go."

"Jeff—"

"I can't have you crying. You can't be a part of this. You're too good. Too perfect."

Her eyes widened. "Perfect? Those words did not just leave your mouth." She sniffed. "We were perfect once, Jeff. We had what few ever have. But we both destroyed that. *Both* of us. I'm far from perfect."

He shook his head. She didn't get it. She was beautiful. Yes, she'd made her own mistakes, but still she was innocent to the horrors of the world. He couldn't taint her with this. How could he get her to see that?

She stood and looked up at him, her eyes still wet with tears but now burning with fire. "I've got news for you. I'm already a part of this. I'm a part of you, and I have been for over thirty years. You have demons? Guess what? So do I. Maybe not as frightening, but they're there. And here's another newsflash. Your demons are my demons. I will never be free of them either. Not until you're free. And you can't be free if you keep them inside. They'll destroy you." She moved closer, touched his cheek. "And I will go down kicking and screaming before I see you destroy yourself."

"Mia—"

"I mean it, Jeff." Her eyes were shooting darts. She slid her hand from his cheek down his shoulder and arm, and then took his hand. "Come with me."

She led him to the living room, sat down on the couch, and patted the cushion beside her.

Jeff knew his face was streaked with tears. He badly needed a handkerchief. But he sat next to her anyway and fell into her arms, the sobs coming again.

Mia held him, smoothed his hair, didn't mind that he was ruining her blouse. He cried and he cried and he cried. For how long, he didn't know. Didn't care. He cried for the years he'd missed with Maria, with Angie, with his niece and nephew. He cried for his grandfather and brother, whom he'd never really known. He cried for the poor boys in prison whose abuse he couldn't stop.

And when he thought he was finally done crying, he cried some more.

Through it all, Maria held him to her breast and rocked gently back and forth, as if he were a child she was comforting.

He wasn't sure how much time had elapsed when he pulled himself together. Maria rose without speaking and brought him a box of tissues. He wiped his running nose. She returned to the kitchen, and he heard the microwave running. A few minutes later, she came out holding a steaming mug.

She handed it to him. "Here. Chamomile tea."

"Herbal tea?"

"It'll help you relax."

"I like regular tea."

"You don't need any caffeine right now. You're strung up enough as it is. This'll help." She patted his hand. "Trust me."

He reluctantly took the cup. "I didn't even know I had chamomile tea."

"It was in the cupboard. Angie probably left it when she moved."

He couldn't help but smile. Like mother like daughter.

"Drink up."

He took a sip. Hmm. Not sweet. Not tea. But all in all not bad. Oh, hell, who was he kidding? It tasted like hot water.

"You ready to talk?" Maria asked.

He drowned in her dark brown eyes. She was so good. So caring. Had been an amazing mother to those three beautiful kids. Could she handle his demons?

As if he'd spoken aloud, she took his hand. "I'm here for you. I can deal with anything you had to deal with. I want to. It's part of you, and I want to know every part of you, Jeff. I always have."

"There were horrors there."

She visibly swallowed. "I know."

"Horrors I never wanted to bother you with."

"I'm here. I'm asking you to bother me. I need you to. And you need to do it just as much."

He nodded. "I was one of the lucky ones." He closed his eyes. Black-and-red images clouded his mind, threatened to pull him in. He mentally pushed them away. "I was big enough and strong enough to avoid the...rapists."

"Oh, thank God." Maria let out a breath. "I was afraid—"

Jeff held out his hand to stop her. "There were nights I wished I hadn't been so lucky."

"What?"

"You don't understand. To be witness to that kind of cruelty. The pain they inflicted..." He shook his head. "I tried to stop it once. I got beaten so badly I spent a few weeks in the infirmary. And the poor boy got it twice as violently because of my interference."

Maria's face paled. She swallowed again. She was trying to hold it together for him. He clamped his hand to his mouth, his stomach churning. How could he do this to her?

"I'm okay," she said. "Go on."

"There was never any quiet. At night, I heard the wails of

the smaller boys who were targeted by the rape gangs. It was..."
How could he describe this? "They'd scream and scream, all
kinds of voices, some high, some deep—but I always knew the
exact time they got penetrated. The scream became a cry for
help. A pleading. The sound was...different, like an appeal. A
prayer. I know that doesn't make sense. And I can't describe
it any better."

She exhaled. "I understand."

But she didn't. She couldn't.

"And the fighting. There was one guy. He was called Big
Chuck. He was there when I got there, and still there when I
left. I watched the man age thirty years, but I swear, he still
looked the same to me. He was a big bear of a guy. Pale and
silvery blond. He looked Scandinavian. His sidekick, Jamal,
was black as coffee. They were polar opposites, but only in
looks. They had the same ruthless taste for infliction of pain
and humiliation."

Maria squeezed his hand harder. He could tell this was
hard for her, but she kept nodding, kept saying, "Yes." So he
went on.

"They were both huge. Chuck was a little bigger. Maybe
that's why he was the leader. Hell if I know. He was also a
little meaner. Though Jamal was one mean motherfucker."
He looked up. "Sorry."

"It's okay. I *have* heard those words before." She gave
him a tentative smile. "Do you think they were gay?"

He shook his head. "Nah. I suppose it's possible, but
I doubt it. Wouldn't have mattered anyway. This wasn't
about relationships or orientation. It was about humiliation,
violence. Besides, to be gay or straight you have to be human
first. These two were animals. The other big fellas either

stayed the hell away from them, like I did, or joined in, depending on how evil they were. The smaller fellas didn't stand a chance. They either allied with one of the larger guys in exchange for protection, or they tried to remain invisible. Some of them were better at that than others.

"I remember this one boy. I don't even know his name. He was small, with feminine features. A beautiful kid. He could have been one of those androgynous Calvin Klein models. He was that pretty. He had blond hair and blue eyes, couldn't have been more than eighteen or nineteen.

"I never even knew his name or what he was in for. They never left him alone. He died within a few months from the abuse."

Maria clasped her hand to her mouth but quickly removed it. "I'm sorry."

"Don't be sorry. It's terrible. You *should* be reacting that way. You wouldn't be human otherwise."

She gazed into his eyes, her own eyes moistening. "He was the one you tried to save."

Jeff nodded, his throat constricting. He cleared it and went on.

"There were others too, of course. Usually the younger, smaller boys, but sometimes the gang would target a bigger one."

"But you..."

He shook his head. "I was one of the lucky ones. I was big enough and masculine enough...and I made the right friends quickly. That was key."

A tear slid down Maria's cheek. "I'm glad."

Jeff looked at the ceiling. "Glad?"

"Of course. I'm glad you didn't have to...go through that."

"You're not understanding, Mia. I *did* go through it. Every night. And the only thing that kept me from trying to stop it again was knowing they'd be all the harder on their victim if I interfered. Trust me, I would have landed back in that infirmary every time if I'd thought I could have made it even a little easier on those kids."

"Oh my God, Jeff." Maria had a far-off look in her eyes, as if knowledge had dawned on her.

"What?"

"You're punishing yourself, aren't you? You're punishing yourself because you couldn't help those men. And because you were spared."

Jesus Christ, the tears again. He'd thought none were left. He dropped his face into his hands.

She understood.

The soothing touch of her hands on his back was a little comfort. But not much. How could he bring her into this hell he lived every day? She deserved better.

She deserved a whole man.

"Shh," she soothed. "Everything will be all right."

How he wanted to believe her—to take her in his arms and lose himself in her lovely body. He'd nearly done so last night.

Instead, he cried in her arms...and relived every stupid decision he'd made in his godforsaken life and every foul day he'd spent in that godforsaken place.

★ ★ ★

Thirty-Three Years Earlier
Jeff stared at a big man he didn't know. His grandpa didn't have

house servants on the premises after five p.m. Who was this guy?

The air thickened around him like an invisible cage. His skin tightened and he held back, quivering. Whoever the guy was, he had a gun pointed right at Jeff.

Jeff held up his hands. "Hey, man, we don't want any trouble. I'm Jeff Bay. Norman's grandson."

"Yeah? And I'm Doris Day."

Trey let out a nervous chuckle. "Funny."

"Shut up," Jeff said, his hand shaking as he reached into his pocket. "I really am. I can show you ID. I visited Grandpa at the hospital today and he wanted me to...uh...get some stuff from his office for him."

"Yeah," Max said. "We're here for the old man."

"Mr. Bay didn't say anything to me."

"Of course he didn't," Max said. "He's in the hospital."

Jeff regarded Max. This was coming really easy to him. Too easy. The lies slid from his mouth like slime oozing from a gangrenous limb. His voice didn't crack once.

Friend? No. Max was not Jeff's friend.

The man shifted, still pointing his gun at Jeff. "I mean Mr. Wayne Bay."

God. That stupid name coming to bite him in the ass again. "Mr. Wayne Bay is my brother." Unlike Max's, Jeff's voice cracked. He cleared his throat. "Why don't you give him a call?"

"I didn't know Mr. Bay had a brother."

Grandpa and Wayne had never even mentioned him? Figured. "Well, here I am. And you can see the family resemblance, I'm sure." Why hadn't they worn ski masks? This was the biggest fuck up ever. And he thought he'd crossed all his Ts on this one. He'd gotten lazy. Lazy and stupid. He should have known Grandpa had hired some kind of night security.

He glanced at Trey. The flashlight was still lit and in his hand, illuminating the floor. An idea sparked in the back of his mind. He motioned his head ever so slightly and then glanced at Max. The three of them had been working together a long time. They hadn't yet faced gunpoint, but they'd gotten out of a lot of bad scrapes by working as a unit. Once the two men were on board, he nodded.

Quick as a flash, Trey raised his arm and shone the flashlight in the security man's eyes. Caught off guard, the man blinked at the light. Before he could respond, Max had karate chopped his arm and the gun spun to the floor.

As it was closest to Max, he rushed to grab it. Things were good, until—

"What the heck is going on in here?"

Taken by surprise, Max picked up the gun and waved it in the direction of the new voice and fired.

At Wayne.

CHAPTER EIGHTEEN

Maria wept with Jeff. If only she could take his pain away, she'd gladly bear it all herself. He had finally calmed down. His handsome face and eyes were swollen and red from crying. She'd never imagined Jeff crying. He'd always been so strong.

But he was human. And he'd been to hell and back.

She understood now. She understood that he'd felt every ounce of pain those poor men had gone through, to the point where he'd wished it were him going through it, because that might be preferable to witnessing it. She understood all too well.

Any mother understood. Thank the good Lord, her children hadn't suffered anything so horrible, but every time they had gone through a difficult time, Maria had nearly died watching their pain and would have gladly borne it to save them the suffering.

She knew she'd never truly understand the horrors Jeff had witnessed and experienced, but she finally understood where his head was.

Could she help him?

She didn't know. But she could be here for him, and that's what she intended to do.

She nudged him. "Come on. You need a bath."

He shook his head. "I don't take baths."

She stood and pulled at his arm. "Today you do. It'll relax you."

His sunken eyes seemed to look right through her, until they softened. "Okay, Mia. Whatever you say."

She led him to the master bathroom and started the water. "I don't suppose you have any essential oils?"

That got a little smile out of him. "Fresh out."

She nosed through the cupboards. "Maybe Angie left something." But no, nothing. Plain water would have to suffice. Didn't matter anyway. He only needed the warmth and the steam to relax his body and mind.

She tested the water and plugged the drain. She wanted it hot but not too hot. "Splash some cold water on your face a few times," she said to Jeff.

"Mia..."

"Did I give you a choice? Go on now." She inhaled. She was starting to sound like a mother here. She definitely didn't want to be his mother. "Sorry. But it'll help. I promise."

He obeyed her and then turned toward her, droplets of water hanging from his unruly hair. Even in the state he was currently in, he still took her breath away. He was the handsomest man she'd ever seen.

"Go ahead and take off your pants," she said. "The water's about ready."

Again he obeyed her and stepped into the tub.

"I'll be right back." She hurried to the kitchen and grabbed a large cup. When she returned, he was leaning back in the tub, his eyes closed.

"Before you get too relaxed, let's take care of your hair."

He sat up, saying nothing. Clearly, he'd decided to go along. She poured cupfuls of water over his head to wet his hair and then massaged a liberal amount of herbal shampoo onto his scalp. She washed gently, massaging, trying to help him relax. A low groan told her she was succeeding. When she'd finished, she rinsed, again with the cup, and dried his eyes with a soft towel.

She squeezed some shower gel on a shower pouf and washed his body, being careful to keep it as nonsexual as she could. He needed comfort right now, not sex. And after witnessing his breakdown and learning what he'd been through, she wasn't much in the mood either.

When she'd cleaned him as best she could, she stood.

He opened his eyes. "Where are you going?"

"Just out to the bedroom. You relax. Enjoy the water. Take as long as you want. Get out when you start looking like a prune."

"Will you stay in here with me?"

She looked around. Only one seat in the house. She sighed and sat down on the closed toilet. "Of course I'll stay. Do you feel like eating though? I could heat up the breakfast I brought."

He shook his head. "Maybe in a little while. For now, just stay. Please."

The toilet was too far away for her to hold his hand, so she got up and sat down on the floor by the tub. He grabbed her hand before she could take his.

He closed his eyes, leaning back. He didn't play with her fingers, just held her hand and breathed in and out— sometimes deeply, sometimes more shallow so she thought he had fallen asleep. But then he'd take a deep breath again.

She had no idea how long they sat there. When he finally moved to get out, she stood, handed him a towel, and then left the bathroom.

When he emerged, naked, he said, "Would you lie down

with me for a little while?"

She nodded. She lay down on the bed, hoping she could offer more comfort.

He lay beside her, spooned up against her. Soon his breathing indicated he had fallen asleep.

Finally, she let herself go and wept.

★ ★ ★

Thirty-Three Years Earlier

Wayne dropped to the floor, clutching at his upper arm and moaning.

"Christ, Max, what have you done?" Jeff lunged toward his friend, grabbing for the gun.

Max dropped it to the floor and Wayne crawled toward it. The security guard ran from the room.

"God, Wayne, are you okay?" Jeff knelt next to his brother, who gripped the gun with a bloody hand.

"No, I'm not okay, you asshole. I've just been shot. What the hell are you trying to pull here?"

Jeff didn't answer. It ought to be clear enough. "Who's that other guy?"

"Regan. Our nighttime security."

"Since when?"

"Since none of your business, Jeff. What are you trying to do, rob us?"

Max walked toward them. "Give me that gun, Bay."

Jeff tried to get a look at Wayne's arm. "Get out of here, Max. Can't you see he's hurt?"

"Tell him to quit being a baby. I just grazed him. It was an accident."

"Let me take a look at it," Jeff said.

His upper arm was bleeding pretty good, but it did seem to just be a nick. "I think you'll live."

"Of course he'll live," Max said. "Let's get the fuck out of here."

Jeff looked around. "Where's Trey?"

Max shuffled. "Didn't you see him? He ran like a chicken shit right after big brother here showed up and got himself shot."

"Shut up. God." Jeff turned to his brother. "Wayne, you're going to have to give me the gun so I can wrap up your arm."

"Oh, hell, no."

"Look. I need to get your bleeding stopped, and then we'll call the ambulance, okay?"

"Ambulance." Max widened his eyes. "Have you gone mental?"

"My brother needs medical attention, you moron."

Max stalked forward. "Give me the fucking gun, Bay."

Wayne, arm shaking, raised the gun, and shot. Max went down yelling, clutching at his calf.

"Jesus," Jeff said, "what did you do that for?"

"I didn't hurt him," Wayne said. "I'm a better shot than that. But he needed to be stopped."

Footsteps trampled down the hallway.

"Shit," Jeff said under his breath.

Within seconds, Regan stood in the doorway, a new gun in his hand. "The police are on their way, assholes."

Before Jeff could stop him, Max had lunged forward on the floor, grabbed the gun from Wayne, and shot Regan.

Dead.

CHAPTER NINETEEN

Maria woke to the smell of ham and eggs. She patted the bed beside her. Jeff had gotten up. He came into the room, smiling and holding the tray she had brought...how many hours earlier? She felt like she'd aged a few years since this morning.

His eyes were still swollen, but all in all, he looked good. The major difference was his demeanor. He looked happy.

And she hadn't seen him look happy in a very long time.

"You were moving around and stretching, so I figured you'd be up soon. Thought you might be hungry."

And she found, to her surprise, that she was famished.

Jeff wore only a pair of jeans. He looked delectable as usual, but she turned her mind away from such a sexual scenario. He might not yet be ready to resume their relationship, and she had to make peace with that. In her heart, she knew they'd be together. Someday.

"I *am* hungry. Thanks. We can take this in the kitchen."

"When I went to all the trouble of reheating this and setting it on the tray and walking twenty feet to bring it in here?" He winked. "Not a chance."

She smiled, hoping she didn't look too horrible due to the tears she had shed earlier after he'd fallen asleep. "Okay."

She sat up and arranged some pillows for their backs. He set the tray in front of her.

She inhaled. "Smells great."

"It ought to. You made it."

"So I did. I hope you like it."

"I already sampled a bit of it. It's delicious." He situated himself beside her and took one of the filled plates off the tray.

They ate in silence. When Maria finished, she moved the tray away and took Jeff's plate. When she started to rise, he stopped her.

"I thought I'd take this stuff out to the kitchen."

"That can wait. Here—" He took the tray from her and set it on the floor next to his side of the bed.

Maria swallowed, unsure what was to come. She said nothing.

He turned to face her, cupping her cheek with one palm. His touch sent her sizzling.

"Mia, I wish I could take parts of today back."

"Jeff..."

"I'm serious. I never wanted to dirty you with any of that."

"Please. I'm a big girl. I wanted you to open up to me."

"I know. And I adore you for it. I just never wanted you to have to deal with any of those things. They're too...awful."

"I want to deal with it. I want to be here for you. And I intend to be."

He smiled, stroking her skin. "There's something I need to tell you."

Apprehension sliced through her. Was he going to set her loose? Say they had no future? That he'd never be healed? She balled her hands into fists. Damn it, she was prepared to fight for what they'd had, what they could have again. She'd give him all the time he needed, but they *would* have a future.

She forced her voice to stay steady. "What is it?"

He smiled. "I forgave you long ago."

She widened her eyes. He had? And all this time...when he was pushing her away... Did he no longer love her? A pit of hopelessness opened in her belly.

He spoke again before she could form any words. "I forgave you. And I forgave Wayne. I'm glad he was there for you and for Angie. You both needed him, and I'm glad he loved my little girl."

"He was her—"

"—favorite," they said together.

"I know she was," Jeff said. "I wish he and I could have made peace while he was alive. But at least I know he was a good man and he took care of all that was precious to me."

The lump in her throat began to dissolve. She was still precious to him. But still he held something back.

"The thing is, I couldn't be with you, even though I had forgiven you."

"Why not?"

"I couldn't forgive myself."

"Jeff, all those mistakes you made were long ago. You were young and headstrong. You had been disinherited. Everyone makes mistakes."

"Mine cost a man his life, and though he didn't die at my hand, I'll have to live with that forever. I thought that was bad enough. But then, in prison, when I couldn't help those innocent boys..."

Maria's heart ached. Jeff Bay was a good man. A truly good heart. "I know."

"I felt I was inadequate in some way. That a better man could have intervened and stopped those atrocities."

"Jeff, you are the best kind of man. You always were. You just lost your way a little. And though you're a good man, you're only *one* man. There was nothing you could do."

He nodded, his eyes distant. "I realize that now. It will take some time to heal, but I'm ready to start the process."

"We can find you a therapist. The best there is."

He chuckled. "In Bakersville?"

She smiled. "Well, we'll have to go to Denver. But I'll go with you. You won't go through this alone. I promise. Harp will give you half a day off. No problem."

"But the cost, Mia."

Hang the cost. She'd gladly pay for the best therapy in the world to heal Jeff. But he wouldn't take her money. She already knew that. Didn't matter though. "Silly, didn't you read those papers you signed when you started working here for Harp? All of our employees are covered with health insurance, and the state of Colorado has mandatory mental health benefits."

Jeff's eyes widened, and he broke out into a loud guffaw. He grabbed her face and kissed her lips. "All this time, Mia, I've been killing myself wondering how to get through this. Do you know I never once considered that I had benefits here?" He laughed out loud again.

And what a joyful sound it was! Maria laughed with him. She hadn't heard that wonderful sound in over thirty years. And all over health insurance.

He pulled her to him, still laughing, stroking her back. "My Mia. I should have known you'd take care of me in the end."

She smiled with him, happiness overwhelming her.

And when his laughing stopped, and he softly kissed her neck, her happiness turned to unglorified glee. She pulled back a little and met his gaze. No words were necessary.

They slowly undressed each other, kissing softly, caressing each other's bare skin. Maria knelt and sucked on Jeff's cock, which felt as divine beneath her tongue as she remembered. She twirled her tongue around the head and then spiraled tiny kisses over the shaft, all the way down to the base, where she licked and cupped his balls. Then back up, where she took him to the back of her throat.

He shuddered. "God, Mia, I've missed you so much."

His words warmed her, spurred her on. She began moving her mouth faster, adding her fist to the mix, wanting so much to feel him explode inside her mouth. So much....

He grabbed her hand. "No, baby. I want to take it slow."

She reluctantly let his cock drop from her lips.

"Let me take care of you now." He laid her gently on the bed and spread her legs.

Maria leaned forward and held on to the sides of his head, her fingers threaded through his silky hair, as he stroked between her legs with his tongue. "Jeff, yes, just like that." He licked her and sucked on her clit, and just when she was about to go mad, he thrust two fingers into her heat and she soared.

That feeling—that amazing feeling—that had been lying dormant inside her for so long awakened again.

He moved forward, covering her body with his, and kissed her deeply. They kissed for a long time, all the while their hands never leaving each other.

And when he finally entered her, time rolled backward and she took flight.

★ ★ ★

Thirty-Three Years Earlier

"Jesus Christ!" Jeff ran to Regan. The shot had gone right into his chest. Blood had already soaked his shirt. Jeff put his fingers against the man's neck. No pulse.

"I am so outta here," Max said, throwing the gun down.

"You just killed someone," Jeff yelled. "What the fuck is wrong with you?"

Max ran out the door. Wayne struggled on the floor.

Jeff's heart thrummed, his whole body aware of its rapid beat. What to do? Get out? Wayne knew they'd been here. He could identify all of them. Max wouldn't get far. Still...if he grabbed one of the cars in Grandpa's garage, he could head south, maybe make it to Mexico...

God, he was thinking crazy. A man was dead. *Dead.* Bitter agony welled up inside him.

He looked toward his brother. Wayne was still struggling for something. Shit! He hadn't wrapped Wayne's wound.

"What are you doing?"

"I'm trying to get my cell phone in my pocket. Shit this hurts!"

"You're bleeding. What the hell do you need your phone for?"

"To call the cops, you moron. You've outdone yourself, Jeff. Even I didn't think you were capable of this."

God damn. Why the hell should he care about his brother's wounded arm? Wayne was about to finger him to the cops. Black rage bubbled in his blood. He was through. Through with these people. Fine. He'd take the heat. What choice did he have? He'd be dragged off to jail and then he'd cop some kind of plea and get probation. Max had killed someone. He hadn't.

He'd take care of this, and then he'd make a life with Mia. A modest life, but a good life. A happy life.

He looked at his brother, hatred boiling in him. "Don't bother with your phone. Regan said the cops are already on their way."

"You won't get away with this, Jeff."

Jeff didn't reply.

"Why did you do it?"

Jeff shook his head and met his brother's gaze. "You're really asking that question? Really? You don't think it's just a little unfair that you stand to inherit everything Grandpa owns and I get squat? Christ, Wayne, I wanted what's rightfully mine."

"And instead of talking to us, you dragged those two dregs of society in here to rob us? You're insane."

"Talk to you? You can't be serious. Neither of you have had a kind word to say to me—"

"Freeze!"

Three uniformed cops bombarded the room, guns pointed.

"Cuff them both," one said.

"Hey," Wayne said. "I live here. This is my house. And I've been shot in the arm."

"And you?" The cop turned to Jeff.

Must be a new cop. Most people in town knew who Jeff Bay was.

"I have no idea who he is." Wayne looked away. "Cuff him and get him the hell out of my house."

CHAPTER TWENTY

Jeff basked in his happiness as Maria cuddled against him, her soft snores giving away her slumber. She was his again. And this time he'd never let her go.

She stretched a little and opened her eyes.

"Good morning, sleepyhead." He chuckled. "Or should I say good evening?"

She smiled. "You doing okay?"

He nodded. "I haven't felt this good in a long time."

"Good. I'm glad."

He looked into her chocolate-brown eyes. "I love you, Mia."

"Oh, Jeff." She wrapped her arms around his neck and squeezed, and then pulled back a little and returned his gaze. "I never thought I'd hear you say that again. I love you too."

He smiled and pushed a stray strand of onyx hair behind her ear. "Thank you for waiting."

"I would have waited forever. There's never been anyone else for me."

"For me either. Only you, my Mia."

She hugged him again, and he held her close. He had a long road of healing ahead, but he knew, in his heart, he'd never have those nightmares again.

★ ★ ★

Thirty-Three Years Earlier

The county jail sucked. Crowded into a dirty cell with the dregs of society, as Wayne called them, wasn't on Jeff's bucket list. What in God's name had he been thinking, living the kind of life he'd been living? Over a week had gone by. He'd lost track of how many days. He'd been arraigned for robbery, but he had no money for bail, so he had to wait until a public defender came to see him so he could make a deal.

Max had been taken in as well. Fortunately, he and Jeff hadn't had any contact. Jeff wasn't sure he'd be able to keep from throttling the guy.

The doctors had taken a sample of his blood earlier today. He wasn't sure why, but he had nothing to hide.

Mia had come to see him a couple of times. He wasn't allowed much time for visitation, and he had to sit behind a glass wall and look at her pretty brown eyes and talk to her on a phone. But at least she had come. At least she cared.

She'd assured him that she knew he was innocent, that everything would be okay, but he got the distinct feeling she didn't believe him. Something in her face, her eyes. Sure, he'd been in trouble before, but he'd never harmed another human being.

He'd get out of this, and she'd believe in him again.

It was late. Visiting hours were over. She hadn't come today.

He inhaled a deep breath and let it out slowly. The public defender would surely come tomorrow. Then this nightmare would be over.

He'd go home to Mia.

★ ★ ★

"Help me, Maria!"

Maria sat up in bed. Meghan? What was going on? "What's wrong?" Maria stood, wrapped her robe around her, and walked swiftly to Meghan's room. She wasn't there. Meghan called again, from the bathroom. Maria hurried in.

"What is it? Are you okay?"

"I'm scared. I'm bleeding."

"Goodness, what happened? Did you fall down or something?"

"No, it's... I think it's my period."

"Your period? Oh my." Meghan was only barely eleven. Pretty early, but certainly possible. "What happened?"

"It was on the toilet paper."

"Are you in any pain? Did it hurt when you peed?"

"No."

"Okay, not a urinary tract infection then. I guess it is your period. I'll get you a pad, okay?"

"I'm scared."

"Honey, this is nothing to be scared of. You're just growing up."

"I didn't expect it yet. None of my friends...you know..."

"Well, you'll be the first then. They'll all be jealous."

That got a smile out of her. "Yeah, I guess maybe they will be."

"Sure they will." Maria groped in the cabinet under the sink for her box of pads. Meghan was too little for a tampon.

"Here they are." She pulled out a pad and unwrapped it. "You just pull off the paper here and it sticks to your panties."

A jolt hit her. Déjà vu. Only it had been...how many weeks

since she'd used one of these? Not being sexually active, she hadn't bothered keeping track, but her cycles were pretty regular. About every four weeks. But her last period had been well over four weeks ago, maybe even five or six.

Oh my God.

She and Jeff had used protection—the second time anyway. But he had pulled out the first time. Not a reliable method. How stupid were they? Truth be told, she hadn't given it more than a thought. She'd been so overcome with desire... *Oh!* She wanted to slap herself. Her skin grew cold. She rubbed her arms.

"Are you okay?" Meghan asked.

She cleared her throat. "Yes, yes. Of course." Her sister was becoming a woman, and she was centered on herself.

But what would she do?

No reason to worry. It was probably nothing. Stress, of course. Jeff had been arrested, and she'd been worried...

God, Jeff had been arrested! A man was dead. He'd be going to jail for sure. For how long, she had no idea.

She wanted to believe he was innocent. In her heart, she knew he was, but even so, he'd been caught red-handed at the scene of a robbery and a murder.

What would she do if she was pregnant?

She inhaled and turned back to Meghan. "Can you handle everything now?"

"Yeah, I think so."

"This is nothing to worry about, Megs. Just a part of growing up. If you have any questions, you know where I am."

"Should I, like, stay inside or anything?"

"No, of course not. You can do anything you want to do. Except swimming. You need a tampon for that, and I think you're probably too young for those. And in five or six days it'll be gone."

"Okay." Meghan walked out of the bathroom.

Maria set the cover on the toilet seat down and plopped onto it. What to do? Her heart skittered. She'd read in *McCall's* magazine about a new home pregnancy test that had come on the market. It was ten dollars. She'd scrape together the money and buy one.

No reason to worry until she knew for sure.

But she had a sinking feeling she already knew.

CHAPTER TWENTY-ONE

Jeff tottered around in the kitchen, looking for something to eat. Maria was asleep in his bed. Where she belonged. He'd closed the door so as not to disturb her when hunger had led him out for a snack.

He glanced at the clock on the counter. Nine thirty. They hadn't left the house all day. Maria had been there since she'd shown up that morning with breakfast.

His Mia. They were together again. *God, so much time lost!* But they were on their way to making up for all of it.

He jerked when someone pounded on the door. *What the hell?*

He went to the door. No peephole. "Who is it?" he asked. Could be Harper. Or maybe one of the hands.

No response.

Well, that's weird. He lived on a private ranch. The knocking sounded again. Perhaps whoever it was hadn't heard him? He wasn't scared, exactly. Still, something whispered to him to leave well enough alone.

He walked away. Whoever was there would get the message. He just hoped the knocking hadn't woken Maria.

And again, the pounding. Jeff's heart stuttered. He had a very bad feeling.

He turned out the light in the kitchen and headed back to the bedroom.

But jolted when the door crashed open.

He blinked, his heart leaping into his throat.

No.

God, no.

It couldn't be.

★ ★ ★

Thirty-Three Years Earlier

Maria's hands shook uncontrollably as she read the instructions to the pregnancy test once more. Nausea permeated her, and she swallowed back a heave. She hadn't eaten anything anyway. There was nothing to come up. She hadn't eaten since she'd had the revelation yesterday, when she'd helped Meghan with her first period. No appetite. Just a perpetual sick feeling from her stomach that flowed through her whole body.

Maybe she'd made a mistake. Maybe she hadn't done the test properly. All those little test tubes and droppers... It would be so easy to screw it up.

Maybe the test wasn't positive.

But it was.

She'd known since she had the thought.

And Jeff was in jail. She hadn't visited him in days. Couldn't bring herself to. God, she loved him more than anything. How could she have fallen in love with a criminal? He'd robbed his own family. She shuddered, her lips trembling. A man was dead. A man was dead because of what the man she loved had done.

And she did love him. More than anything. What did that say about her?

They'd made a baby together. Created a life. A life that

was now growing inside her. If Jeff weren't in jail, they'd be celebrating right now. Sure, the timing wasn't perfect. She'd have to put off college. But a baby...

An innocent life. A sweet little baby who deserved better than she could offer. Better than a young and broke trailer trash mother and a criminal father.

The baby deserved the name and life she was entitled to.

A solution came to her. Maria knew what she had to do.

She just hoped she had the courage to do it.

★ ★ ★

She'd showered and spent two hours making herself as beautiful as she could. She didn't want to. But she had to. She wore a denim miniskirt and a hot pink tank top that slid up to show just a sliver of olive skin between the pink and the blue waistband of her skirt. Her legs were bare and on her feet she donned a pair of high-heeled blue leather slides she'd borrowed from Shelley. Now she stood outside the big barn on the Bay ranch. A leering ranch hand had looked her over, nearly salivating, and had finally told her this was where she would find Wayne.

She'd seen him before, a couple of times in town. Shelley had pointed him out. Wayne was attractive, of course. He was Bay stock. But his dull brown hair couldn't compare to the ebony that was Jeff's. And his eyes were mousy brown, not dark and burning like Jeff's. His face was nice, but not as chiseled and perfect as Jeff's.

Basically, he was good-looking, but he wasn't Jeff, and he never would be.

But he had the Bay name, and he had the Bay genes.

And damn it, so would her baby.

Maria wasn't a seductress by nature. Her only real experience had been with Jeff. But for her baby, she'd do what she had to do. Her baby—and Jeff's—would have the name and future it deserved.

She took a deep breath and entered the barn. Wayne stood at the far end, currying a gorgeous brown mare. His left arm was still bandaged from the skirmish nearly two weeks ago now. Who had shot him? Jeff had said his pal Max had done it. She believed him. But...oh, it was just such a mess. Everything had turned upside down. She loved Jeff so much, but right now, her baby was the most important. Maria had to do right by her child.

She walked forward and cleared her throat.

He looked up at her and smiled. "Well, hi there. Who might you be?"

"I'm Maria, Maria Gomez. My family lives in town."

"What brings you out here to Bay Crossing?"

"Well..." *God, Maria, get a grip.* "I heard you're the man to see for the best peaches on the western slope."

"None better."

"I'd like to get some for my mother. I hope it's not too late. She loves peaches, and she's been ill and can't get out to get them herself."

"Oh? I'm sorry to hear that."

"She'll be okay. It's not serious. But I couldn't let her go without her peaches."

"So how'd you hear of us here at Bay Crossing?"

"How could I not have heard of you? You're the best."

He smiled again, wider this time. "Well, the peaches are almost gone. But I might be able to scare up a bushel or two for someone as pretty as you."

She warmed. This felt all wrong, but at least so far her plan was working. "That's a beautiful horse."

"Thank you. Her name is Mahogany. Do you ride?"

"Only a little. I grew up in town, not on a ranch."

"Maybe we can go riding sometime. Mahogany here is really gentle. She'd be good to you."

"I'd adore that. When can we go?"

"Anytime. For you, I'll make the time."

Perfect. She inhaled and then leaned into him, faking a swoon. His arms went around her to keep her from falling.

"Are you okay?"

She sank her cheek into the soft fabric of his shirt. "I'm fine. Just a little lightheaded. I'm...on a new diet and I'm a little hungry. It will pass."

"You? On a diet? Whatever for? You're already gorgeous."

She smiled what she hoped was a seductive smile and raised her fingers to his cheek. *Dear God, I'm going to get struck down by lightning for this.* "I'm so happy to hear you say that. And I hope you don't mind me saying that you're the most handsome man I've ever seen."

He grinned sheepishly. "Maria, I don't mind at all."

CHAPTER TWENTY-TWO

Big Chuck slammed Jeff against the wall next to the door, a gun pointed at his neck.

"Why the fuck didn't you answer the goddamned door, Bay, huh? Not expectin' callers this time o' night?"

Jeff closed his eyes, his heart stampeding, his bowels going into overdrive. *Please, let Maria stay asleep through this, whatever happens. Please don't let her come out here.*

"Did you miss me, you stupid fuck?" Chuck jammed the nose of the gun farther into his neck, against his Adam's apple.

Jeff fought the urge to choke, and his blood turned to ice. "How the hell did you get out?" he rasped.

Chuck let out a laugh. "Seems I know some people in high places. Course I had to wait it out. I got out a month ago, and funny thing—I ran into a guy, and your name came up."

"What the hell do you want with me? I did my time. You did yours. We're both free men now."

"True that. The problem is, no one really wants to give a con a break, you know? I got no money, got no job, no chance of employment. And I don't really want to do any decent work anyway. So I found a way to make some quicker money so I could hightail it to Mexico."

Jeff fought to maintain control. *Keep him talking. And keep him talking low, so Maria won't wake up.* "What do you need with me, then?"

The other man spit on the floor. "Seems someone is

willing to pay pretty handsomely to see you dead, Bay."

Jesus Christ. He didn't have any enemies. Maybe someone from the slammer? But he'd minded his own business except for that one time, and Chuck and Jamal had already taken their revenge for that.

Oh, God.

The name came to him in a red haze. *Max.* Max was freaked and was willing to have Jeff killed to make sure he didn't squeal him out. God, he'd given the dumb fuck his word. Why would Max send this maniac after someone he used to call a friend?

"How'd you find him, Chuck?" Jeff asked. "How'd you find Max?"

"Ah, so you figured it out. Funny thing is, if I got the story straight, you did the dumb fuck a favor all those years ago, takin' the rap for him."

"Yeah. No shit."

"But now he's afraid you're gonna send the heat after him as some kind of payback."

Jeff clenched his gut. "I already told him I had no interest in that. I just want to get on with my life."

"I guess he don't believe you, Bay."

"Look, Chuck, you need money? I got money. Way more than Max can give you." He didn't, but his family did. He could get money if he needed it. They'd lend him some. He was sure of it.

"Yeah?"

"Yeah. I'm not lying. You see this ranch all around you? My nephew owns it."

"You got any here?"

"Here? In the house? Of course not." Jeff closed his

eyes, and a weight dropped inside him. *Bad move, Jeff. Really bad move.* How could he have made such a stupid mistake? Goddamned nerves.

"Then that don't do me much good, does it?" Chuck poked him again with the gun. "That Max fella put a bounty on your dead head, and I aim to collect."

Shit! Keep him talking. Keep him talking.

"I'm thinkin', though, that before I blow your brains out, I might finally take a taste of that sweet ass of yours."

Bile bubbled in his throat. *Oh, hell, no.* He hadn't escaped Chuck and his thugs for thirty years to be raped now. He gathered all his strength and tried to break Chuck's hold.

To no avail. The man was just too big and too strong. He stood about six-six and had to weigh three fifty. He'd ruled by size and meanness in prison, and he would do so again outside.

Chuck nudged the gun farther into Jeff's neck, catching his Adam's apple again. Jeff let out a wheeze.

"Dumb ass. You really think you can get away from me? Your friends aren't here, Bay. It's just you and me now."

Jeff breathed in, trying to slow his racing heart. All he could manage was a short puff of air.

Chuck squeezed one globe of Jeff's ass with his free hand. "You're a prime specimen, Bay. It's been so long, I may never go back to women. If I do, I'm going back door. Nothing like a tight virgin ass."

Nausea bubbled in Jeff's throat, and his bowels clenched. But damn it, a rape would be better than getting killed. Now he had something to live for.

"Drop your pants, shithead," Chuck said.

Jeff's fingers shook as he unbuttoned the snap of his

jeans and then slowly rolled the zipper downward.

Chuck stopped him. "On second thought, I think you'll suck my dick first." He forced Jeff to his knees. Keeping the gun at his neck, Chuck worked his own snap and zipper.

Jeff resigned himself to his fate.

Nothing had changed. He was a free man, but he was in a new kind of hell.

He swallowed the nausea and closed his eyes. He'd do what he had to do.

And then, the voice of an angel.

"Put that gun down and slide it across the floor, you sick fuck."

★ ★ ★

Thirty-Three Years Earlier

"God, Mia, you haven't been here in so long. I've missed you. How are you? Are you okay?"

His first thoughts were for her. Her well-being, when he was the one locked up.

"I'm...okay. How are you?"

"Been better. But I'm finally going to meet with the public defender later today. Then we'll get things going. I might get a few years for the robbery, but I hope not. I... God, Mia I'm so sorry. I wish I'd never done such a stupid thing."

She nodded. "I know, Jeff. But you did." She regretted the words as soon as they left her mouth. "I'm sorry."

"No, I'm sorry."

A few seconds of silence passed. Maria gathered her courage. She had to tell him. She'd made a decision for the good of her child. There was no turning back.

She bit her lip. "I'm not sure how to tell you this."

"Go ahead, Mia. You can tell me anything."

She sobbed into a tissue. "I love you."

"I know you do. I love you too."

"But I did something terrible, Jeff. And I know you won't be able to forgive me."

"I'd forgive you for anything."

"Not this."

"Just tell me. I'll understand."

"Oh, Jeff, how did it all come to this? You behind bars, waiting for some stupid public defender? I don't understand."

"I made a mistake. But I'll tell the truth and I'll pay my dues. And then we'll be together."

Maria shook her head. "I'm afraid we won't be."

"What?"

"I... I did the unforgiveable."

"Lay it on the line, Mia. What are you talking about?"

"I slept with your brother."

★ ★ ★

A giant anvil hit him in the gut. If he hadn't known better, he'd swear he'd just been sucker-punched.

"You what?" No, not Mia. Not his sweet, beautiful Mia.

"And..."

"Fuck, there's an 'and?'"

"I'm pregnant." She gulped. "With Wayne's baby."

Jeff went numb. Maria continued to speak. That is, her mouth moved, but all Jeff heard was white noise inside his brain. Muffles of whizzing fans and whirring engines. He stood, his legs acting on their own. And he left Mia standing there, the phone still in her hand, her cherry-red lips still moving.

"You done, Bay?" the guard said.

"Yeah. I'm done." He cleared his throat. "I need to talk to my attorney."

"Yeah? He just got here."

"I'm going to cop a plea."

Two days later, the cell doors locked for Jeff Bay. Permanently. He'd pleaded guilty to felony murder. Because he'd copped a plea, he was spared the death penalty. Bummer. At the moment, he'd welcome the blackness of nothing. But nope, it was life imprisonment for him. If he was lucky, he might be eligible for parole by the time he was sixty.

It was no less than he deserved for how he'd lived his life. He had drugged his brother and seen him shot, and a man was dead because of a crime he'd participated in. Yet for Mia, he'd have gone straight, made good, done what he could to make up for the havoc he'd wreaked.

But Mia was no longer his.

He flopped down on his bunk and said good-bye to life as he knew it.

To Grandpa Norman, who had disinherited him, taken away his future, and to Wayne, the backstabber.

To his unborn niece or nephew.

And to Mia.

Good-bye.

CHAPTER TWENTY-THREE

Maria held her ground. Inside, her body shook with tremors, but outside, she was ice-woman. She had to be. Jeff's life depended on it. No way would she let anyone hurt him ever again.

The big man glared at her, the gun still pointed at Jeff.

"I'm not kidding," she said, willing her voice not to crack. "I'll shoot your ass. Now drop the gun and kick it over to me."

"Who the fuck are you?" the man asked.

"Does that really matter? I'll blow your brains sky high if you don't do what I say. This is your last chance. Kick the gun over here."

Seeing Jeff in that submissive position—on his knees before this maniac—terrified her, but damn it, she would be strong. She would not cave like she had all those years ago, running to Wayne.

"Who is she, Bay?"

Jeff stayed quiet.

"I asked you who she is!" He nudged the gun into Jeff's neck.

Maria cocked her gun. The big man turned. Good. He'd heard it. "This is your last chance. I don't give a rat's ass if you die right here and now."

The big man finally moved the gun from Jeff's neck and set it on the ground.

"Slide it over."

He complied. She didn't dare bend down to pick it up. Her heart leaped into her chest, and she fought the urge to burst into tears of thankfulness.

Now what? The big man could easily overpower Jeff.

But quick as a flash, Jeff was up, with Angie's old replica of David's head in his hands. He beaned Chuck on the side of the head with the statue, a dull thud sounding. The man fell into a heap in the entryway.

Maria ran into Jeff's arms. "Oh God oh God oh God." The tears came. "I was so scared."

"That makes two of us." His arms tightened around her. "All I could think of was you. I prayed that you wouldn't wake up." He pulled away for a minute and gazed at her. "Now I'm glad you did."

She gulped. "We better get him tied up or something before he comes to."

"Yeah, right. There's some duct tape in the kitchen." Jeff glanced over at the bust of Michelangelo's *David* on the floor. "Grandpa kept that in his office. I always hated the damned thing, but I'm sure glad it was here."

"Wayne gave it to Angie." Maria's voice shook. "She never liked it either. Said it was in poor taste to copy an original. I guess that's why it's still here."

Jeff walked to the kitchen and came back with the duct tape while Maria quickly dialed 9-1-1 and explained the situation.

Jeff bound Chuck's wrists and ankles. "He won't be moving now."

Maria burst into tears. She hated herself for it. She wanted to be strong for Jeff, but—

"It's okay." He wrapped his arms around her. "Where did

you get that gun?"

"There's a secret compartment in the bedroom. It's at the foot of the bed. There's a loose floorboard. Wayne insisted Angie learn how to use a gun and have one in the house if she needed it. She never took Wayne seriously, but she acquiesced and did learn how to use the thing. Thank God she never had to use it in real life. I had a hunch she might have forgotten about it when she moved. Thank God, she did."

"Yeah, thank God."

"Do you know how to use it? Would you have shot him?"

She nodded, still shaking. "Wayne insisted I learn to use a gun too. I have one just like this one in a similar floorboard hiding place in my bedroom."

He clasped her to him. "You're the bravest woman I know."

Still shuddering, she clung to him. "I guess we're even," she said, "because you're the bravest man I know."

He hugged her tighter. "Yes, Mia. Together, there's nothing we can't overcome."

★ ★ ★

A couple of hours later, the police had been and gone, and Chuck was carted back to prison. Jeff had told the police the whole story, and they put out an arrest warrant for Max.

Maria collapsed on the couch beside Jeff. "What a day!"

Jeff sighed. "You're telling me. If I never find myself staring down the barrel of a gun again, it'll be too soon." He clasped Maria's hand in his.

A phone buzzed from the kitchen.

Maria stood. "That's my cell. It's in my purse in the

kitchen. I'll just be a minute." She hurried to the kitchen and grabbed the phone out of her purse. Angie.

"Hi, sweetheart," she said into the phone.

"Oh, Mama, thank goodness." Angie sounded out of breath. "You'll never guess what we found!"

Maria's heart hammered. She'd had more than enough excitement for one day. "Is everything all right? Is the baby all right?"

"Yes, yes, Little Jeff is fine. As you know, though, we're doing some remodeling of the old house, and they just started taking out the big wall in the master bedroom."

Angie was always changing things or moving things. She'd done it since she was a little girl. The old ranch house at Bay Crossing was beautiful just as it was. Maria had lived there herself with Wayne and the kids until she'd inherited Cha Cha from her great-uncle and the family had moved east. But leave it to Angie, always having to have her way. Maria smiled into the phone. Angie was just Angie, and Maria wouldn't have her any other way.

"Yes?"

"So they're taking out the drywall, and guess what they found inside the large back wall?"

"I couldn't possibly guess."

"A safe."

A safe? Something niggled in Maria's brain. Wayne had mentioned a safe once—that his Grandpa had kept behind on old Impressionist painting in his bedroom. But by the time Wayne and she moved into the house, the safe gone.

Or rather...drywalled over.

"Do you know the combination, Mama? Did Daddy ever tell you?"

"No, he didn't, Angie. We didn't even know the safe was still there."

"We'll pull it out of the wall and take it somewhere to have it opened," Angie said. "I can't begin to guess what might be inside."

"Whatever's inside belongs to your brother and sister as well as to you. And to your Uncle Je— Er, your father."

"Of course, I know that, Mama." Angie scoffed. "You give me so little credit sometimes."

"I'm sorry, sweetheart. Sometimes I forget how much you've changed in the past couple years. I couldn't be more proud of you."

Jeff walked into the kitchen. "Is everything all right?"

"Yes, it's Angie," she said to Jeff. "Hold on a minute, sweetheart," she said into the phone. She turned to Jeff. "You'll never guess what happened. They found your grandfather's old bedroom safe while they were tearing down walls."

Jeff's mouth dropped open. "You mean, you never knew about it?"

"No, I did. Wayne told me, but by the time we moved into the house it was gone. Turns out your grandfather built a wall over it. Wayne just assumed he'd gotten rid of it. Angie's going to take it to a locksmith to have it opened."

Jeff smiled. "She doesn't have to. I know the combination."

★ ★ ★

"I can't believe your grandfather walled that safe up," Maria said.

"He must have gotten a little weird in the head at the end," Jeff said. "Did Wayne ever say he was going senile or anything?"

"As you know, he died a few years after Wayne and I got married, and I never noticed anything strange. If Wayne did, he never mentioned it, other than to say he was always a little weird in the head."

Jeff thought for a moment. Then, "Grandpa definitely had his own way of doing things. He hated banks, so he kept most of his cash in the house in two safes in his office. No one ever knew what was in the bedroom safe. Until now."

"That explains the stock certificates," Maria said. "He wanted them in his possession rather than in an account somewhere."

Jeff nodded. He couldn't believe it himself. The safe held sixty-year-old stock certificates in an electronics company that had split so many times they were now worth millions. Plus ownership interests in several silver mines throughout Colorado.

But that wasn't the real treasure. For Jeff, the ultimate riches lay in the will dated a few months before Grandpa's death, giving Jeff back his inheritance, along with a letter, handwritten by his grandfather, forgiving him. Why Norman had walled up the safe and decided not to make the new will public, Jeff would never know, but at least he knew his grandfather had been *thinking* about forgiving him. That meant the world.

He took Maria's hand and looked into her dark eyes. "Mia, I love you."

"I love you too, Jeff. So much."

His heart warmed and he said the words he'd been waiting to say for thirty-three years.

"Please, be my wife. I don't want to waste another minute of the second chance we've been given."

EPILOGUE

Maria looked into Jeff's eyes as they finally separated after a deep and passionate first kiss as husband and wife.

Therapy was going well. Jeff had been going twice a week for two months now, and Maria had joined him for a few sessions. They both had a lot to work out, not the least of which was their recent run-in with Chuck, who was back behind bars, as was Max. She looked around at their small gathering. Angie and Rafe with Little Jeff, now two months old and just starting to smile. Harper and Amber, who had recently announced their own good news. And Catie and Chad with eighteen-month-old Violet. Catie's two brothers-in-law, Dallas and Zach McCray, were also there with their families, and Amber's father, retired bronc buster Thunder Morgan. That was all—a perfect small wedding.

The minister laughed. "Now that the bride and groom have managed to unclench, I am happy to present to you Mr. and Mrs. Jefferson Bay."

The applause was thundering. She and Jeff smiled at each other and then walked down the aisle...toward their life together.

MESSAGE FROM HELEN HARDT

Dear Reader,

Thank you for reading *Tantalizing Maria*. If you want to find out about my current backlist and future releases, please like my Facebook page: **www.facebook.com/HelenHardt** and join my mailing list: **www.helenhardt.com/signup/**. I often do giveaways. If you're a fan and would like to join my street team to help spread the word about my books, you can do so here: **www.facebook.com/groups/hardtandsoul/**. I regularly do awesome giveaways for my street team members.

If you enjoyed the story, please take the time to leave a review on a site like Amazon or Goodreads. I welcome all feedback.

I wish you all the best!

Helen

ALSO BY HELEN HARDT

The Sex and the Season Series:
Lily and the Duke
Rose in Bloom
Lady Alexandra's Lover
Sophie's Voice
The Perils of Patricia (Coming Soon)

The Temptation Saga:
Tempting Dusty
Teasing Annie
Taking Catie
Taming Angelina
Treasuring Amber
Trusting Sydney
Tantalizing Maria

The Steel Brothers Saga:
Craving
Obsession
Possession
Melt (Coming December 20th, 2016)
Burn (Coming February 14th, 2017)
Surrender (Coming May 16th, 2017)

Daughters of the Prairie:
The Outlaw's Angel
Lessons of the Heart
Song of the Raven

ACKNOWLEDGMENTS

Tantalizing Maria, the long-awaited seventh book in The Temptation Saga, tells the past and present story of Angie's parents, Maria Gomez Bay and Jeff Bay. Its structure is a bit different from the previous books in the series, and I hope you enjoy it.

So many people helped along the way in bringing this book to you. Thanks so much to my talented editors, Celina Summers and Michele Hamner Moore, my eagle-eyed proofreaders Tanya Kaanta, Amy Grishman, Scott Saunders, and Chrissie Saunders, and to all the people at Waterhouse Press—David Grishman, Meredith Wild, Shayla Fereshetian, Jonathan Mac, Kurt Vachon, Yvonne Ellis. Your expertise and guidance are most appreciated.

Thank you to my amazing street team, *Hardt and Soul*, for your endless support of my work. You're the best!

And thanks most of all to you, the readers, who clamored for more Temptation Saga! The series ends here...for now.

ABOUT THE AUTHOR

New York Times and *USA Today* Bestselling author Helen Hardt's passion for the written word began with the books her mother read to her at bedtime. She wrote her first story at age six and hasn't stopped since. In addition to being an award winning author of contemporary and historical romance and erotica, she's a mother, a black belt in Taekwondo, a grammar geek, an appreciator of fine red wine, and a lover of Ben and Jerry's ice cream. She writes from her home in Colorado, where she lives with her family. Helen loves to hear from readers.

Visit her here:
www.facebook.com/HelenHardt

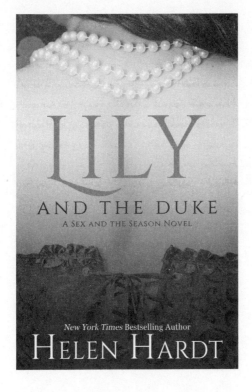

CHAPTER ONE

Laurel Ridge, the Lybrook Estate, Wiltshire, England, 1845

Lady Lily Jameson set down her portable easel and palette of watercolors to smooth her mussed sable curls. The September day was sweltering, and beads of sweat trickled down her face. She gazed around the small alcove that appeared to be the remains of an old stone chapel. The long grass tickled her ankles under her skirt. White and yellow daisies poked cheerful heads through the lush green foliage, and yellow and magenta blooms dotted the abundant vegetation like confetti. A tiny brook babbled nearby.

Lily sighed, hoping she could capture the beauty of the alcove in watercolor before her mother and father noticed she was missing from the afternoon lawn party.

She tied on her painting smock, set a piece of thick cotton paper on the easel, and coated it with water. She started with the bright cerulean of the sky, and then the brook and the rich greenery behind it.

"That's quite good."

Lily jumped up, knocking over the small tin of water sitting in her lap. She turned and stared up into a golden face and striking green eyes. Her breath caught.

"I'm sorry," the young man said. "I didn't mean to frighten you."

"No, I'm fine." Lily, trembling, wiped her stained fingers on her apron.

His hair was the color of ripe wheat, and it fell to his shoulders in gleaming layers that brushed the collar of his brown jacket. He was tall—taller than her father or her brother—and his broad shoulders led down to slim hips and legs clad in tight tan trousers and brown riding boots. He wore no cravat, and a few tawny hairs peeked out of his crisp linen shirt. His face was handsome, with a strong jaw, full lips, and a Grecian nose. Long mahogany lashes adorned his arresting eyes.

Lily swallowed. Something new and uncomfortable churned in her stomach. Like butterflies. Or rolling water.

"How did you come to be here?" the man asked.

"I-I wanted to paint."

He smiled, revealing straight white teeth. "My mother likes to paint. I find her here often."

Lily clenched her clammy fists in her stained smock. "Your mother?"

"Yes. My mother. Your hostess. The duchess."

"Oh." Lily widened her eyes and willed herself not to stammer. "You're the marquess, then?"

"No. The marquess is my older brother, Morgan. I'm Lord Daniel Farnsworth." He smiled again. "And who might you be?"

"Lily, my lord." She offered a quick curtsy.

"Lily who?"

"Lady Lily Jameson."

"You're Ashford's daughter?"

"Yes, one of them."

"Is the other as pretty as you are?" he asked, winking.

Warmth crept into Lily's cheeks, and she hoped the young lord didn't notice. Imagining her blond-haired, blue-eyed sister, she said, "More so, I think."

"That, I doubt." He cleared his throat. "You have quite an eye for painting. I shall leave you to your work. I'd love to see it when you're finished."

"Yes, my lord."

He turned to leave, but looked over his shoulder. "How old are you, Lily?"

"Thirteen, my lord."

"Be sure to come back in five or six years," he said, and walked lazily out of the alcove.

Continue Reading in Lily and the Duke

Visit www.helenhardt.com for more info!

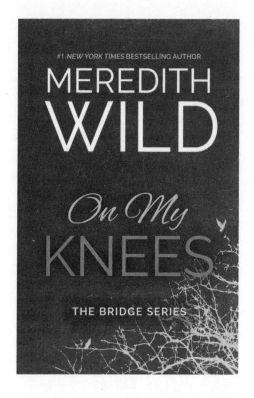

Keep reading for an excerpt!

CHAPTER ONE

I startled at a sudden knock. Only one person could be at my door. I checked the clock again. He was early. I hadn't expected that. I got up from the bed, tossing my book to the side. My heartbeat sped, and I straightened my white sundress, my one decent looking dress. I pulled the elastic band out of my hair and let it fall loose down my back. I fussed a minute longer until he knocked again. Energy and excitement coursed through me, and I took a deep breath before opening the door.

There he stood, almost too gorgeous to be real. I released the doorknob and found my other hand, twisting my fingers in tremulous anticipation. He looked different. His familiar blue eyes bore into me, but the Texas sun had darkened his olive skin. He appeared at least twenty pounds lighter. The strong lines of his jaw and cheekbones were sharper. Between that and his nearly black hair, trimmed into a short crew cut, he looked older. I should have expected changes in his physical appearance, but an irrational fear tempered the flood of emotion that rushed over me at the sight of him.

Did he still feel the same way? Could he have changed this much on the inside too?

Struggling for the right words, I opened my mouth to speak. His lips quirked into a small smile, setting off a relieved one of my own. He stepped in and caught my fidgeting hands in his, rubbing his thumbs over the white of my knuckles until I relaxed. The warmth in his eyes melted away any lingering fears. I exhaled a shaky breath.

"Come here," I whispered, still afraid to break the silence and unable to do justice to how overwhelming being in his presence again was.

I stepped back, pulling him after me. He followed and once inside curved his arm around my waist, tightening his hold until we were firmly chest to chest. My body molded to the hard lines of his. My breaths came fast, my entire body responding to his closeness. His bright blue eyes bore into me, locking me in. He traced my lips with the pad of his thumb, his smile fading as he did.

"I missed you so much, Maya. Every day..."

Out of habit, I hooked my hand around his nape. I mourned the overgrown locks that would have tangled between my fingers, but none of that mattered now. Changed or not, he was here. His heart, the heat of his body pressed against me. This was all I'd wanted. My love in the flesh. It all felt like a dream. Maybe I'd wished for him so hard and for so long that somehow he'd come true. The separation had been almost unbearable. I couldn't—wouldn't—consider how we'd face it again.

"I can't believe you're really here." My voice wavered.

He feathered his fingertips over my cheek, calming me. I released a tentative breath. I went to kiss him, but before I could meet his lips, he stilled me, gently cupping my cheek.

"I love you," he whispered, his soft breath dancing on my lips.

My heart twisted, a bittersweet ache pulsing through my chest with each beat. We'd written it, said it so many times, worn it out. The profoundness of those words from his lips, now, nearly knocked me down. My entire being warmed from the inside out. Possessed with a fervency to prove how much I felt it too, I lifted to my toes and kissed him. Our lips met, then our tongues, tangling, teasing, and tasting.

"Maya," he breathed, breaking our contact with the words.

"What?" I got lost in his eyes, never wanting any of this end. I'd never loved him more. My soul was brimming for everything I felt for this man.

Continue Reading in On My Knees

Visit www.meredithwild.com for more info!